Broken Heart Trail

Broken Heart Trail

M. J. SMITH

Morning Joy Media

Spring City, Pennsylvania.

Thank you to Angie Batluck for her insightful quote choices and to Karen Heard for her creative cover design. Thank you to my family and friends for their love, support, and encouragement.

Published by Morning Joy Media.

Visit www.morningjoymedia.com for more information on bulk discounts and special promotions, or e-mail your questions to info@morningjoymedia.com.

Cover design: Karen Heard | Chalk Design
Interior design: Debbie Capeci

Smith, Marijo.
    Broken Heart Trail / by Marijo Smith.

Summary: When the consequence of a foolish choice interrupts their romantic vacation, Dan and Deb Gallagher are separated. As Dan wrestles with both physical pain and haunting memories, Deb begins the grueling trek for help. Her subsequent disappearance and the specter of a skier with questionable motives raise the stakes during the feverish search in subzero temperatures.

    ISBN 978-1-937107-19-2 (pbk.)
    1. Abduction—Fiction. 2. Pennsylvania—Fiction. I. Title.

Printed in the United States of America

To Meme, my loving and supportive grandmother

Chapter 1

The woods are lovely, dark and deep.
—Robert Frost

This can't be the right trail. I've been cross-country skiing for years, and I've never seen an intermediate trail this difficult, even in the White Mountains. I think we're lost.

I stopped for a minute to look around and then turned to my wife. "Deb, I think we took a wrong turn somewhere back there."

"We followed the map and this trail is marked as blue, Dan. That's how the other intermediate trails are marked."

"I know, but this incline is too steep, and there are way too many switch backs. We must be on an expert trail."

The White Mountains are majestic and serene. There's nothing like being out on a cold day skiing in a place surrounded by white. It's an ideal setting for a winter adventure, which this has turned out to be, but in the wrong way.

For about ten minutes, we tried maneuvering the hill on our skis doing a sort of side-step technique called the herringbone, but the incline was too difficult for us. For every step I took, I slid back three. Frustration set in, and I sat down on the side of the trail being careful not to disturb the groomed area, although it didn't look like anyone had used it in quite some time, and who could blame them? It was an exhausting climb. I used my ski pole to unlatch my right ski and then my left. I sat for another few minutes waiting for Deb to catch up. She was busy taking her skis off, too.

Looking back at the portion of the trail we just scaled, I determined it was definitely a black trail. In cross-country skiing easy trails are marked by a straight green line, intermediate trails are marked by blue bunny hills, and difficult trails are marked by black steeply jagged lines. Just looking at that symbol on a map made me want to steer clear of the expert trails. I took a cross-country ski class or two in my time, but I was no expert. The classes I took taught me how to bend on my knees and lean into a turn. They taught me how not to mess up the groomed area, which is the area of the trail that has the ski track already set in it. Imagine a wide path covered in snow. The outer edges of the path have ski tracks, which are made by machine. The middle of the trail is used for doing the herringbone, which was another useful technique that I learned in my classes. Skillfully maneuvering an expert trail was not covered in any of my Cross Country Skiing for Dummies classes, except that unless you are an Olympian, stay off the trails marked in black.

Something else not taught in these classes is that there is always some part of nature to appreciate when on a cross-country ski expedition. The view from the top of the hill was spectacular, and it made me forget about the tough time that Deb and I were having. Most of the trees were still snow-covered, and from my vantage point I could see the top of Mount Washington and its weather station towers. It was ten below zero when we left at nine o'clock this morning. We'd been out for about an hour, but it didn't feel any warmer. Deb covered all exposed skin; she chose warmth over vanity. It took some convincing this morning, but Deb finally agreed to wear goggles and a scarf, which she had since pulled up over her chin and cheeks. Even though it was bitter, fresh New Hampshire air just can't be beat.

Deb and I have taken a few ski vacations in the two years we've been together. We just got married last July and now here it was February in the Presidentials. When I first introduced this sport to Deb, we had just started dating. It was a little after Christmas.

Before Deb and I were together, I used to go on great skiing trips with friends. Some of the best excursions were with downhill skiers. I always loved the line, "Oh, I didn't realize you had to *walk* so far in cross-country skiing." Once they went out a few times, they soon came to love the peace and solitude. When we were all single, we went on many expeditions together. I guess that's why I enjoy this. Every time I ski it's an adventure. I get to experience new places in a different way, and being in the deep forest in the winter brings a wealth of joys—the snow bunny tracks, the birds gathering their food. No matter what is going on in my life, seeing the birds in the frigid, snow-covered forest helps me remember that God provides food, warmth, and shelter for them. He will provide for me, too, and I know I can get through tough situations. Like right now. Even though we're lost, we'll get through this just fine. There were other people out on the trail. I could hear the murmur of a snowmobile in the distance. We also passed a few interesting people skiing this morning. There was a woman in her fifties out here alone. She skied with determination and intensity, probably starting a new chapter in her life. We were on the same path going in opposite directions, and only a few years ago I was in her place, out here alone.

We also saw a man on the trail a short time ago. Deb and I were skiing up a hill on a true intermediate trail right before we took the wrong turn. Both of us were focused on the ground in front of us instead of watching where we were going. I felt a strange sort of presence at the top of the hill, and when I looked up there was a man staring at us. He had a wild, unkempt mountain-man look to him with long crazy hair sticking out of his hat. He wore a flannel shirt over all of his layers and sweatpants over, I hope, long underwear. It was too cold for just a flannel shirt and a pair of cotton sweatpants. First of all, any spill would result in soaked pants and ten below zero was not the weather for wet cotton. But what was even stranger is that he was wearing the best skis and ski boots that money could buy. It just didn't fit. If he was the type of skier who would put money into equipment, then why not invest in some clothing that would protect him from the elements instead of making him susceptible to them? As he skied down the slope toward Deb and me, she looked nervous about being in the way, but I told her she was fine. A rule on the slopes is that people coming up the slope get out of the way of people going down. It's much more difficult to dodge people at the high speed reached going down a hill than it is when at the bottom slowly climbing up. Deb was far enough out of the mountain man's way, but she still had a look of apprehension as he passed us. I was irritated because he stared us down, and we weren't doing anything wrong, so I stared back at him, and he met my gaze with an icy look. Usually people out here were friendly; this was one of the first times that someone made me feel uneasy, but that feeling went away as the trail became more and more challenging.

Yesterday's skiing had been much better and much easier—forty degrees of pure delight. It was Valentine's Day and the lodge we were staying in sponsored a champagne and chocolate ski in which skiers followed a pre-mapped route. Hearts were stapled to trees along the route where there were stations set up with chocolate and champagne. Although it was a nice idea, Deb and I opted to go it alone. We took a variety of beginner and intermediate trails and saw many hearts along the way. We counted the number of hearts to figure out how tipsy the other skiers might be by that point.

On our map was a little notation about a tent where the ski patrol kept refreshments, so we decided to swing by. They had hot chocolate, hot cider, and water; the perfect complement to some of the snacks in our backpack. The tent wasn't heated, but it was much warmer inside than out and we had a nice, relaxing break. That's how we ended up lost today. We didn't want to take the same trails as yesterday, so we plotted a course that would bring us to the tent from the opposite end of the ski resort.

We brought apples with us and we were both getting hungry. We were tempted to rest along the trail and eat, but our goal was the tent and the apples and hot chocolate would be our reward for our hard work. It's just that it was much colder than yesterday. The temperature change from forty degrees to ten below made the snow a little slick. This expert trail was not marked so our map didn't do us any good, but I was confident that we would find our way out. We always did.

Deb finally made it to the top with me. "Deb, it's a beautiful view from up here."

She was a little out of breath, but she managed to say, "Getting lost might just have been worth it with this view."

We continued to take in the stark contrast between the snow-covered trees and mountains set against the blue sky.

Deb shivered.

"Here, take my coat. I'm warm enough."

Deb declined, "Thanks, babe. You keep your coat, though. I actually feel pretty good, considering. We should probably figure out where we are and head back. I've been reading some books from the library at the inn, and there have been a lot of people who have died up here—most of them because of the cold. I just hope we're not too far away from the lodge. There aren't many people out today, and we expected to be at the tent by now warming ourselves."

"You need to stop reading that book. We're fine. We're dressed warm enough for the weather and I think I know where we are."

"Where are we?"

"An expert trail," I said with a slight grin on my face.

"Very funny, Dan. I'm still trying to breathe normally after climbing up that hill."

"It'll be easier going down." Both of us laughed, still trying to get a few more minutes of rest in before we had to start our trek out.

Deb sounded relaxed, but a little concerned, "All joking aside—which expert trail? I kept looking back down the hill as we were walking up, and I don't think I would be able to ski it. It was hard climbing up; those hills are steep and there were some sharp turns that I don't think I would make it around. And now that we are at the top, this other side doesn't look any better. There is a steep slope that turns sharply to the left. It's almost in the shape of a backward L. That turn has got to be impossible to make. I wouldn't even want to walk it if it were covered only in grass. It's a dangerous trail."

"I think we're on the Ptarmigan Trail and you definitely don't have to ski down. No bets or races today."

"Agreed. There's no way I am going to freeze *and* break my leg on the same day. No way, no how."

"You're not going to break your leg and we'll be back in the warm lodge in no time. No worries—this is vacation."

As I locked my boots in my skis, Deb said with a half laugh, "Oh, you're not going to ski down this hill." It was more of a demand than a question.

My response? I turned to Deb and said, "I'll try anything once." Big mistake.

———

I'll try anything once. That's something you say when someone wants you to try sushi for the first time. *I'll try anything once.* That's something you say when your girlfriend wants to go to the opera and you just want to appease her knowing that this "anything once" will land you a night at a ballgame with the guys. *I'll try anything once.* That had always been my philosophy, so I stood at the top of the hill and dug my skis into the snow. It was too icy to get a good grip with my skis, but I thought the hold I had was good enough. *I'll try anything once.* I started down the Ptarmigan Trail and after about four feet I wished I were on a tether line, a bungee cord, anything really, and it was the last time I thought *I'll try anything once.*

That moment in my life was a contrast. The sun reflected off the snow in the trees, and the ice crystals on the ground made my surroundings look like someone was holding a prism up to the light. The colors danced around me, and it looked as if I was in a field of diamonds. On that side there was beauty; on the other was fear. In the few feet I traveled, I felt out of control. I picked up speed and no amount of flailing or dragging my poles across the ice slowed me down. Dread rose like a wave in my stomach with its rhythmic rise and fall. I knew something bad was going to happen; I just didn't know what and how bad. In a split second I evaluated the hill. If I kept going straight there was the sharp, backward-L curve at the bottom that Deb was terrified of. I couldn't see around it, but I knew I wouldn't make the turn at this rate of speed, and if I went over the edge, I would plummet into a bed of jagged rocks. It was too late; I was headed for a tree and the last thing I wanted to do was hit it full body. I fell on purpose to slow myself, but the tree didn't move out of my way. I slid all over the trail trying to dig my poles, hands, skis, anything into the icy covering to reduce my speed. Nothing gave me a grip. I hit the tree with my left leg and the force of it lifted me off the ground. The contact I made with my leg sent it bending over my shoulder in a sickening sort of way, and I could make no other sound than that of the wind being knocked out of me.

I remember a few isolated moments about the point of impact. My leg bending over my shoulder and flopping back to the ground as if dead. And *my calm.* And Deb standing at the top of the hill screaming, "Dan, are you okay?" It was a voice I never heard from her. It sounded like a combination of fear and hysteria, a deep guttural scream, and I wanted to answer her, but I just couldn't find my voice. I looked back at her and she said, "Dan, Dan, I'm coming down. I'll be right there. I just need to take my skis off."

I watched Deb unlatch her skis in what seemed like slow motion, but I knew that she was moving faster than my mind processed the information. It must have been only a few seconds before Deb took her skis and put them under her arm, sat on the ground, and slid down the hill on her rear end.

She tried to suppress the terror in her voice, but there was still a hint that she was going to lose it any second. I guess she didn't want to scare me, but it was too late for that.

"Dan, what's wrong? What hurts?"

"I broke my leg."

"Oh, no. Are you in pain?"

"I can't feel anything right now."

"Can you move?"

"I can move. Let me see if I can stand."

"No, don't do that. Just stay where you are. I'll go for help."

"Wait."

"What do you mean, 'wait'? I need to go now or you'll freeze."

"Just wait a minute. Let me see if I can stand."

"You can't stand, Dan. Your leg is broken."

"I don't want a rescue team coming for me if I can make it back on my own. Give me a minute."

"Are you crazy? Let me just go…"

I didn't hear the rest of what Deb said to me. I grabbed onto my ski poles, took a deep breath, and tried to hoist myself up. I put all of my weight on my right leg. I thought this just might work until I put some pressure on my left leg and fell back onto the ice.

"Did you hurt yourself even more?"

"It won't take any weight. I'll need the rescue team."

"I'll go. I'll go as fast as I can."

"Deb, wait. Maybe the cellphones work."

Digging in the backpack Deb said, "I completely forgot about the phones." She pulled both of them out of the inside pocket and held them up. "There's no service. We're too far out. I need to go *now*."

"Just take it easy. I don't want you getting hurt."

Deb's voice took on a calmer tone, "I'll be fine. Don't worry about me."

"I do worry about you. Take one of the phones. Maybe you'll get service closer to the lodge."

Deb reached for the phone and gathered her skis. She stopped, turned, and looked at me with regret, a look I had never seen before, and then she took off her coat. With a soft voice she said, "Here, take this. Slide it underneath you so that the cold doesn't go right through you."

I lifted myself up, and she slid her ski jacket under me. It wasn't the time to be too proud, but I felt bad that Deb didn't have anything to protect her from the cold. I was glad for the coat, however, as it acted as a barrier between me and the ice and I was much more comfortable having this to sit on.

"You'll be okay, Dan."

Deb picked up her skis and a moment of panic hit me. I yelled after her, "Be careful. I love you." I watched Deb run down the rest of the hill without turning around, skis and poles under her right arm. The only sounds were the crunching of her boots breaking through the thin layer of ice and the distant drone of a snowmobile. Soon, Deb disappeared around the corner that she was too afraid to try on skis.

———❖———

I looked my watch. 10:30. Probably wasn't the smartest thing to do—now I'd be tempted to check it every minute. I knew it would take Deb a while to get back to the lodge, but I hoped it wouldn't take too long. Deb wore gloves and a scarf, but the pullover was for skiing in warmer weather. I felt guilty that I had Deb's coat, but it kept the cold from seeping through my lower body. I hoped the cellphone worked closer to the lodge so the ski patrol could pick Deb up, too, and get her someplace warm.

Sitting in the middle of the woods, I had no idea the long road ahead of me. I tried to think of all of the good things. The break was not a compound fracture. Deb would have fainted if that had happened. So that's one good thing. The sun was shining. That's two. Even though I was under tree cover, I managed to fall in the one spot where the trees allowed the sun to shine through to the ground. I turned my face to the sun, and it made me feel better. And, of course, Deb. She's number one on my list.

I looked at my watch again. 10:32. I needed to keep my mind occupied on something other than the time. Turned out after reading that book Deb's concerns about the dangers on Mount Washington were quite prophetic. I understood her preoccupation. Yesterday it was forty degrees, last night the temperature dropped to minus thirty, and this morning it was minus ten. What happens in weather like that was dangerous—the snow starts to melt in the forty-degree weather, and then as the temperature drops that layer of water turns to ice on streets, sidewalks, and snow trails. We dressed much lighter yesterday than we did today. We didn't have our heavy coats, and we would have frozen to death had we been out here all night. If this accident had happened last evening, our story could have been added to that book.

I needed to stop torturing myself, so I looked at my leg and realized the impact of hitting the tree tore my ski pants open. I had thermals on underneath and those were unscathed. I examined my leg and felt the swelling under my hands, but couldn't feel my hands on my leg. Panic set in. What if this was the beginning of paralysis? I tested my body. I moved my right leg, twisted my torso, swung my arms around in circles like we used to do in gym class when I was a kid. It was just my left leg. This gave me hope. I began to think I could walk back to the lodge myself. If I figured out some way to brace my leg and prop myself up, I was sure I could make it back to the lodge. I took Deb's jacket and I wrapped it around my leg. The poles served as my hoist and my stabilizer. It took every ounce of strength I had to stand on my right leg, but I was unsure of how to proceed. I tried this before, and it didn't work. My mind wasn't ready to accept that I was seriously injured. I was always the one to help others. People needed my help, not the other way around. Thoughts of doing even more damage prevented me from moving forward. Defeated, I sat back down on the ice, took Deb's jacket from around my knee, and slid it back under myself for protection. The ability to resist every temptation to look at my watch failed. 10:35. Five minutes since I last saw Deb. It felt like half an hour. There had to be a better way to pass the time.

Chapter 2

*A man should look for what is, and not
what he thinks should be.*
—Albert Einstein

Deb and I first met at the tail end of my summer vacation in the parking lot of our local food store. As I left the store, I spied a lady in distress parked next to me; she had locked her keys in her car. She looked beautiful in her helplessness. Well, she wasn't that helpless. She was trying to reach her hand inside the small space of the cracked window with no luck. This was my chance to be a knight in shining armor. I said, "Did you lock your keys in your car?" So she wasn't going to think I was a brain surgeon, but I couldn't think of anything else to say. Deb smiled and replied, "Yes."

"Do you have a roadside assistance card?" I asked.

"No, but I will after this."

"I have one. You can use my card." *I am such a hero.*

"No, I couldn't do that," she said.

"Yes, you can. I insist."

Looking relieved, she replied, "Thanks."

I called emergency road service for her, and we talked while waiting for the locksmith to get there. "Are you from around here?" *Another great line. A little rusty. I've got to start being smoother than this.*

She said, "I just moved here from Atlanta."

"I've lived here all of my life. Hi, I'm Dan." *Much better.*

She reached out her hand, "I'm Deb. Thank you for your help. With the stress of moving, I just wasn't thinking. On second thought, I was thinking too much. That's why I locked my keys in my car."

"What brings you to Pennsylvania?"

"I work for a theater company, Curtain Call Productions, and they transferred up here. I'm not sure why. There was plenty of business in Atlanta."

"What kind of theater do you do?"

"Mostly, we use short stories, classics like Poe, and turn them into plays. Then we travel around the country performing them for schools. It's a lot of fun, but it's difficult to make any roots. I've lived all over the country, and just as I was thinking Atlanta would be my home, all of the actors got called into a meeting to tell us we were moving our headquarters. I was a little thrown off guard and I considered finding another job, but I really like acting, so here I am."

"I'd love to see one of your plays."

"Well, I'd love for you to see one of my plays, but unless you are a student in high school or a teacher, it's an impossibility."

I extended my hand. "Mr. Daniel Gallagher, physics teacher extraordinaire." *All of the kinks are worked out. I'm getting better at this.*

I waited for the road service to rescue Deb, although it felt like I was the one rescuing her when I handed my membership card to the locksmith. Deb thanked me and went on her way, and probably never thought she'd see me again, but my brain was already in overdrive. There was an English teacher who owed me a favor.

<hr />

Nancy and I have been teaching together for a few years. Our school is stretched to its limits and the overcrowding meant Nancy was stationed in my room. This was the first time in my teaching career, all fifteen years of it, that I would have to share my room and I was not happy at all. I don't get English teachers in the first place. I believed they all thought they were smarter than the rest of us with their fancy language. Sure, I speak English too, I just don't understand half the words some of them use. I do understand the difference between *affect* and *effect*, and I know that *you* doesn't take an "s" in the plural. That's one of my pet peeves, *yoose*. I suppose that's how it would be spelled. Oh, that and *like*. If I had a penny for every time I heard *like* out of a student, I would like be living like comfortably in like the Caribbean right now.

The first in-service day of the year, Nancy walked into my room and said, "Hi, Dan. I'll be using your room this year, as you probably already know. I'll keep my class away from your precious Bunsen burners, and I'll wash the boards after I use them."

As irritated as I was that I had to share my room, I knew this must be more of a pain for Nancy. She had to lug all of her text books and supplies from location to location all the while dodging students in the hallway. I exchanged any desire for sarcasm and giving her a hard time for a bit of compassion, so I smiled and said, "Welcome to E 202, Nancy."

That school year got off to a good start. Nancy kept her word and my room was cleaner than even I kept it. Her only annoying habit was greeting me each day with "Good morning, Roomie!"

Nancy teaches American and British literature, so I knew no matter what stories Deb's group would be performing, they would fit Nancy's classes somehow. One day when class was over, I asked Nancy if she had heard about groups that traveled around the country and performed classic stories for schools.

"Question, have you considered taking the students on a field trip this year?"

"I do like to take students at least one place, but you know how the school board looks at field trips. They think it's a waste of time; the students aren't learning."

"We both know that's a bunch of garbage. They just think we're not really working on those trips. Field trips are fun for students—they can't possibly be learning if they're having fun, and we can't possibly be working if they're having fun."

"You're so cynical Dan."

"Thank you. Anyway, there's a group, Curtain Call Productions, and they will be at the Performing Arts Center next month. It's close and cheap."

"Dan, what are you up to? You've never been this concerned about whether or not the English Department takes students on field trips. Come on, what's the catch?"

"What do you mean?"

"Oh, come on, Dan. You always bust on literature courses and English teachers."

"No, I don't, Nancy. I can't believe you would say that."

"Dan, you get mad every time one of us corrects your grammar. Do you remember that one time at lunch when you said your students were very 'digilent' in completing their assignments and you really meant 'diligent' and all of us laughed? Do you remember how angry you were?"

"I wasn't angry, Nancy. I was disgusted. Disgusted with myself for butchering a perfectly wonderful word."

Now that I had Nancy laughing, I slipped in a lie and reminded myself that once all of this was over, I really needed to tell the truth all of the time. "You got me, Nancy. I just want to prove a point to the school board; you know, show 'em that field trips are valuable. There aren't many places to go for physics, but I know there are a lot of places for English teachers to take students. I know you always take your students to the Renaissance Faire in October because so many of them miss my class, but what about going to see a play for a change?"

I handed Nancy the information for Curtain Call Productions that I secretly took from her mailbox the day before. *I'm hoping that's not a felony.* "Here, the secretary must have put this in my mailbox by mistake."

"So let me get this straight. It would be acceptable for my students to miss your class for a play but not for the Renaissance Faire?"

"That's a good one, Nancy. No, I just thought I would help you out."

Nancy read over the pamphlet. "You know what? I'm up for a good play. If you get all of the information and do all of the paperwork, we'll see what happens. Maybe I'll let you chaperone with me so you can 'prove your point to the board.' Until then I'll let you keep thinking that I believe you."

Am I that transparent? I tried not to change the expression on my face. "That's all I ask of you, Roomie." *Roomie? What's wrong with me?*

After Nancy left, I had five minutes before students filled up my classroom. I took advantage of this time to find the website, but just as Curtain Call Productions appeared on the screen one of my students who tried very hard in my class ran up to my desk, "Mr. Gallagher, Mr. Gallagher, that homework you gave us last night was impossible."

"Not for me!"

"Very funny."

I asked, "Did you do it?"

"All but one problem. The question about waves. I am so frustrated that I'm really starting to dislike the ocean."

"We can't have that. Pull up a chair and let's see what we can do to make you like the ocean again." Sorry Curtain Call productions, you'll have to wait until I get home.

———⋅✦⋅———

And wait I did until I finally got through to a human being only to hear, "Curtain Call Productions, will you please hold?" So, I'd have to wait a little longer. Up until meeting Deb, I never thought about one woman or about settling down to this degree. I guess I hadn't met the right woman. I really didn't want to hang out in bars; I reserved that for my early twenties; besides, I didn't want to hear the gossip about Mr. Gallagher visiting the local hot spots. Not exactly model teacher behavior. So, the bar thing was out. So was the teacher thing. I mean, we have some very nice ladies who teach at the high school, but most of them are a lot younger than I am or are either married or about to be married.

I heard a click on the other end of the phone and a voice said, "Are you still there?"

"Yes, I am. I would like information on production dates in the Reading, Pennsylvania, area."

"Let's see. We have one date scheduled for December fifth."

"That's three months away."

"If you need something earlier, we will be in Philadelphia at the end of November."

"No, thanks. That won't work. Could you send me information at my school?"

"Sure, I just need your address."

Three months is going to be a long time to wait.

———•◦•———

"Three months until the play?" Nancy asked as she wrote the day's assignments on my chalkboard.

"Yeah, is that too late in the year?"

"I don't think so. It should work. Do you have the information?"

"Right here."

"Let's see, the group will be performing some of Twain's and Poe's short stories. We will have read both of those authors by December in my American Lit class. This is perfect.

27

Thanks for finding this, Roomie, even though it really is self-serving."

"Why don't you believe me Nancy? I'm just trying to help."

"I'm not sure who you are trying to help, but this will certainly be a benefit to the students. Remember your end of the bargain—fill out the paperwork and submit it. Make sure to put your name down as a chaperone."

"Thanks, Nancy."

"Can you think of any good reasons, just in case I'm asked, why a physics teacher should come along to a play?"

"Tell the administration that I want to set a good example for the students. I want to show students how important English, literature, reading, and those two authors really are."

"Um, by 'those two authors' you mean Edgar Allan Poe and Mark Twain?"

"Yeah, them. Anyway, what better way than a science mind to demonstrate that? It will be a sort of cross-curricular thing."

Nancy rolled her eyes at me. "Somehow I think just telling admin that you want to prove a point to the school board would be a better option. So, when are you going to tell me why you really want to go?"

Nancy and I have known each other for a while. There are a lot of people on staff who gossip, who even make up total lies about each other, but Nancy is not one of them. She is one of the few people I know I can trust, so I told Nancy the entire story, and this was her response: "Why didn't she just give you her number in the first place? Why the game? I hate to say it, Roomie—what if she was just letting you down easy?"

Did I also mention that Nancy is painfully honest? *Letting me down easy.* That's a thought that never occurred to me.

"Not a chance, Nancy. We're talking about Dan Gallagher here."

———————

Over the next couple of weeks Nancy's words crept into my mind every once in a while. I never considered that Deb might not have wanted to give me her number. I just thought she was being coy.

I considered my situation. I get up at five thirty every morning, go into work by six thirty, spend my day teaching and grading papers. Then I come home. Maybe I'll shoot some hoops in the evening or spend some time with Mark. Mark's a great best friend, don't get me wrong; I just don't want to spend the rest of my life with him.

Embarrassment. Loneliness. Which is the lesser of two evils? I decide loneliness. At least I can hide that. If things don't work out at the theater, everyone will know my embarrassment. On Monday I will tell Nancy I'm not going. She'll need to find another chaperone.

———————

"Good morning, Roomie." This was the part of sharing my room that I was really starting to dislike. Nancy startled me every morning with that phrase. I would sit drinking my coffee in peace and quiet, just enjoying the little bit of time I had without chaos. Then Nancy barges in and disrupts my whole morning. The only thing that made me feel better today was getting this weight off my shoulders by telling Nancy that I wasn't going to be a chaperone.

"Good morning, Nancy. How was your weekend?"

"Great! I visited my sister on Saturday, and I went shopping at the King of Prussia Mall on Sunday. How was yours?"

"Great, as well. Listen, I've been doing some thinking about chaperoning the play."

"Oh, Dan, thanks for reminding me. I have good news for you. I received the signed paperwork from the principal late Friday. I came looking for you, but you had already left."

Nancy extended her hand to me and said, "Congratulations. You're in, Roomie. You're my chaperoning partner. Aren't you excited?"

I faked a smile. "I'm pumped. Gee, thanks for all of your help Nancy." *You're stuck now, big boy.*

"Not a problem. That's what Roomies are for."

I was just going to have to suck it up. If Nancy weren't standing in front of me, I'd have struck the Mr. Universe pose, but I settled for reminding myself that I'm Dan Gallagher...*I'm Dan Gallagher...I'm Dan Gallagher.*

The months passed by slower than usual. It might have been because the weather was unusually warm for November and early December. We didn't have even the hint of snow. Finally, the dreaded day arrived, and Nancy commented first thing, "Good morning, Roomie. Today is your big day. Today could be the first day of the rest of your life."

"I thought English teachers hated dumb clichés like that."

"Oh, but this one is so apropos."

"There's another one." *I'm really not in a good mood. I think my tone gives it away.*

"Roomie, methinks you're having a bad day."

"That's a sad attempt at Shakespeare."

"It couldn't have been too bad, you recognized it as such."

"Stop torturing me with English stuff. I'm going to have enough of it today at the play. What time are we leaving?"

"The buses will be waiting in back of the school where they drop the kids off in the morning. The students are meeting us there at nine o'clock. It doesn't take long to get to the Performing Arts Center, but we're supposed to be early for registration."

"I'll be there." Then after a few seconds, I add, "With bells on."

"Forget the bells. Did you bring a packed lunch since we won't be back in time for the cafeteria's food?"

I looked around dumbfounded, "Lunch? I was supposed to pack my lunch?"

"Ha, ha, very funny."

"What, do you think this is my first time chaperoning a play?"

"Actually, Dan, yes, I do. Relax. Everything will be fine."

The hour and a half until we left was miserable. Students kept running up to me saying, "Mr. Gallagher, Mr. Gallagher, are you going on the trip today?"

"Yes, I am."

"Cool."

We'll just see how cool it is when I'm at the theater. I concocted a plan to prevent any sort of humiliation that might befall me on this trip. *Hide.* That's it. Very simple. Make myself invisible. *I'll be the invisible man.* We are talking about a theater here. Their business is to hide the audience, after all. They make it as dark as possible so that everyone involved thinks they are witnessing reality. It won't be too hard to put my plan into place. I was feeling much better about the whole thing.

As we approached the theater there was a long line of students from other schools standing out front.

"Nancy, are we late?"

"No, they're just really early."

The bus driver dropped us off at the door, and Nancy talked to a theater official. I could tell that he was important; he was holding a clipboard. The official told Nancy to check in at the box office inside. The lobby wasn't as full of students as it was out on the sidewalk. Nancy took full advantage and walked through the lobby to the theater doors just as an usher opened them. She gave her name and we proceeded inside to more ushers who were waiting to receive us. I heard Nancy say, "Sir, could you give us a seat up front?" Oh, great. She is unbelievable. We arrived later than everybody else, and somehow instead of sitting in the very back of the theater, we were on a trek to the front row, a few measly feet in front of the stage. The farther we walked down the aisle, the deeper my stomach sank. We were so close to the stage that if the pit weren't in front of me, I could've touched it. Other classes started filing in and I could just imagine what the other chaperones thought about us. They were the ones who were waiting a lot longer, but we were the ones with the good seats. Any other time I would be thrilled.

I looked around. Funny, but the lights hadn't gone out yet. I slouched down in my chair; part one of my invisible man plan. The student next to me looked over, slouched down in his chair, and closed his eyes. I sat up and tapped him on the shoulder. He got the hint. I had to set an example of good theater behavior. So much for part two of my thwarted plan.

As the ushers closed the lobby doors, the lights remained on. That's odd. From stage right a figure appeared and said, "Ladies and gentlemen, welcome to Curtain Call Productions' performance of those classic pieces of literature that you all loved reading in class."

There was a bit of sarcastic laughter, mostly from the students. I wasn't laughing at all. It was Deb. Of all of my luck. I started to sweat and I just wanted to get as far away as possible. Never look back. My little inner voice kept reminding me in that self-deprecating way that it had, that this whole thing was my idea in the first place. Now here I was in the first row, my plan coming to fruition. The lights were still up and Deb was standing on stage talking to the audience. *Could this get any worse?* Yes, she spied me.

Chapter 3

How much of human life is lost in waiting!
 — *Ralph Waldo Emerson*

I heard skis in the near distance. Fifteen minutes had passed by. Deb might be back at the lodge or maybe the cellphone picked up service and she was able to call for emergency, but either way it was impossible for the rescue team to be here in that short amount of time. Through the trees I saw the figure of a man. He moved at a good rate, but I still was able to glimpse a flash of yellow from his feet, which meant he was wearing professional, skinny speed skis. My skis looked huge compared to his, but I needed mine for home where we don't have groomed trails like this. The man paused at the top of the hill, and I yelled up to him, "There's someone down here."

"Okay, I see you."

"Be careful, it's icy," I yelled back.

The skier took the hill with ease, slowly working his way to me. If only I could have done that.

"Are you all right?"

"Not really," I said, straining my neck to look up at him.

He lifted his goggles and said, "I'll go for help."

"No, that's okay. My wife is on her way now."

"What happened?"

"I lost control on the ice and slammed into this tree. My leg is broken."

"Are you warm enough?" he asked, glancing at the coat under me.

"For now."

"This can be a nasty trail."

"My wife and I got lost and ended up on it. I didn't see it marked as an expert trail."

"It's actually a trail we use for Olympic training. Not many people come up here. It's a good thing you had someone with you."

Olympic training. We really shouldn't have been on this trail.

"Listen, is there anything I can do for you now? Are you thirsty?"

"No, I have water with me, but thanks."

"I really hate to leave you. I feel so bad just going away."

"Don't worry about me. Like I said, my wife is probably at the lodge right now. Go enjoy your day. It'll be nice to know at least someone is."

As he lifted his goggles back over his eyes, he said, "Take care of yourself."

I watched him disappear around the corner, just like I watched Deb. Knowing this man was out here, I wished Deb had stayed with me. He could have gone for help instead, and I wouldn't be worrying about Deb having no coat.

I resisted the temptation to look at my watch for a few minutes, but it was useless. I glanced down and saw that half an hour had passed by. I rationalized the passing of the time with no rescue; I figured it took Deb fifteen minutes to get to the lodge, a couple of minutes for the patrol to warm up the sled, and then the travel time to get to me. I listened for the sound of snowmobile engines, straining to hear anything, when finally the revving of a sled broke through the chirping of the birds. I grew hopeful as the sound came closer. The ski trails were farther away from the snowmobile trails so the only reason for one to be all the way out here was for rescue. I was so relieved to know that soon I would be warm and with Deb, but as my anticipation rose, the sound of the engine seemed farther off than it did just a minute ago. Confused, I looked around trying to see through the trees. Why was the sound going away from me?

Discouragement set in; I realized the distant engine might be coming from the plane flying overhead. *It sounded so close.* I had kept positive up until now, but I was getting colder. The chill reached my bones, and I felt like a little kid who wore blue jeans to go sledding. The cold, wet denim sticks to the skin and there is no way to get warm. Staying outside only makes the chill worse. It's okay while you're sledding, but the walk home is torture with each step as the stiff, half-frozen denim scrapes your leg. *I want to be home now.* I took Deb's jacket out from under me and wrapped the ski coat around my shoulders to give me added warmth. To help pass the time I rummaged through the backpack and found two apples that might give me some needed calories. As I took out the apples, something fell onto the ice. My heart sank and a wave of panic came over me. The trail map. *Deb doesn't have the map.* How was she going to get back to the lodge? Maybe this was why it was taking so long. With so many people staying inside because of the frigid temperatures, finding someone for help would be a challenge. Deb's a smart woman; all she had to do was follow the Mount Washington Hotel, which was visible from most of the trails we had been on these past two days.

Perhaps the ski patrol was having problems and Deb was just fine. I took some comfort in imagining Deb sitting in front of the big stone fireplace in the middle of the lodge, sipping a cup of hot chocolate while the rescue team tries to get the sled started.

It had only been half an hour and that really wasn't that much time. I just needed to relax. Help was coming. I took a few more bites of the apple, and it wasn't until I started to eat that I realized how hungry I was. I concentrated on the apple because when I finished I would have to start thinking about something else to keep from focusing on the pain and cold. I tossed the core over the ledge into some brush. It occurred to me that if the tree had not stopped my fall, I'd be down there instead. That's a positive. I would have been mangled in some horrible way if I had gone over the edge.

Looking back at the top of the hill, I analyzed just how stupid this decision was. *I'll try anything once.* I need to change that philosophy. What made me think that I could possibly make it down the hill and around the sharp turn? I've taken a few skiing lessons. Big deal. That doesn't make me an expert.

I studied my watch again. Forty-five minutes. Now I couldn't stop shaking. I was freezing and there was no getting warm. The early stages of hypothermia; I had no control over the shivering. No matter how hard I tried, I couldn't get it to stop. I had to get indoors. Was it that difficult to have the rescue sled ready? You'd think they would have a policy in place for scenarios like this. I know rescues occur more with downhill skiers, but this place isn't exactly flat. There are tough trails out here where people could get hurt; speaking of which, I was really worried about my wife. What if the delay wasn't because of the resort and Deb was lost out here? I hoped she was okay and wasn't freaking out. She was calm when she left to go for help, but her voice sounded different. I played back my accident in my head. I remembered hitting the tree and then hearing Deb scream. I couldn't answer her because I was in shock at what I had done, and then she screamed again, fear in her voice. I've never heard that sound before, and I hope I never do again.

It had been an hour and the sun lowered behind the pine trees. I wondered if I could slide back to the lodge. The downhill parts would be easy; it was the straight-a-ways that might give me some trouble. I tried to grab my ski pole, but my hands and arms shook and I couldn't hold onto it. How long before I was really a mess? I relaxed the best I could.

Off in the distance I saw a yellow hat through the trees. Another skier. He skied up the hill like a pro, but then he should be if he was on this trail. When he got closer I said, "Help is on its way," and he replied to me, "I am your help."

Oh, thank you, thank you, God. All of that thinking I did just wasted away. Then, I heard the engine of the rescue sled coming closer.

"I'm Bruce, and I just need to check you over." He put his hands on my shoulder.

"I broke my leg. I think everything else is okay. I'm just freezing."

Bruce opened a pack of hand warmers, "Here, hold these."

The heat penetrated my hands and that alone made me feel better. The sled raced around the corner and if I could've stood I would have done a victory dance, I was so happy. Two men got off of the sled carrying a board and blankets.

"How are you doing, sir?"

"Fantastic now that you're all here."

"We'll get you fixed up and out of here. My name is Mike and my partner is Craig."

"I'm Dan. Thank you. I was getting worried."

"We haven't lost anyone yet. You're in good hands."

The three of them checked my back and neck, and then they stabilized my leg. They put me on the board and carried me to the sled. They piled blankets on me and tucked more hand warmers into the blanket for some added warmth. Bruce said, "I'll take your backpack with me. I'll put your skis and poles on the sled and meet you back at the lodge."

"Thanks, Bruce."

"No problem."

I was looking forward to seeing Deb. "Bruce, how is my wife?"

"I'm not sure. I didn't see your wife."

"Oh, I thought she was the one who reported my accident."

"No, she didn't tell me. I was out here patrolling the trails when one of the workers in the lodge called me and told me about your accident and where to find you. I knew the sled was on its way, but I was closer and I wanted to check on you."

"Oh."

"Don't worry, you'll see her when we get you back to the lodge." Bruce must have seen the look on my face, though, because he yelled, "Hey, Mike."

"Yeah?"

"Did you see Dan's wife back at the lodge?"

"No. Craig, did you?"

"No, I didn't either."

My heart welled with dread, but I asked, "Who sent for help?"

Mike answered, "Some guy who came across you on the trail. He said he was worried and couldn't get you out of his mind, so he came back to the lodge and asked if we had helped the skier with the broken leg. We had no idea what he was talking about, so as you can imagine we were concerned. We got here as soon as we could."

My voice filled with the same fear I heard in Deb's voice when I asked, "Has anyone seen my wife?"

Bruce, Mike, and Craig looked at each other and responded, "We need to get you back to the lodge."

All I remember about the ride back to the lodge was staring at a blue sky. That's all I could see from my vantage point. I had never been on a snowmobile, but I can tell you that being dragged on a sled behind one while freezing with a broken leg wasn't much fun.

I just didn't get it. None of them saw Deb. I was sure it was a lack of communication. These guys only get the call to go out; I'm sure there's a hierarchy. I didn't see any of them back at the lodge before Deb and I ventured out this morning. There were only women working at the counter. Deb probably talked to one of the women. I felt the sled come to a stop, but I couldn't get a read on where we were. I was stuffed in too tight. Mike and Craig removed their helmets and walked over to me, "How are you doing, buddy?"

"Okay."

"Sorry if the ride was bumpy. We tried to take it slow and keep you comfortable."

"Thanks, it was fine. It was my first time on a snowmobile."

"Well, I hope it's your last in this condition. Listen, we're going to lift you out of here very carefully, and then we're going to carry you into the lodge, warm you up, and assess your condition a little more thoroughly."

"Okay, thanks."

As they untied the straps and unwrapped the blankets, I tried to get a glimpse of Deb. I didn't see her. There were a few people walking around us looking annoyed that this rescue sled was blocking their direct line into the lodge. I wanted to yell, "So sorry that I broke my leg, people. At least you have that option of walking around me. I don't."

Mike and Craig hoisted me up in a fireman's hold. I had my arms around their shoulders and they each had one of my legs. They asked, "How are you? Is this okay?"

"It's fine," I said, ignoring the pain.

They led me into the main room of the lodge and I looked at the fireplace hoping to see Deb warming herself like I imagined; there was a family sitting near it, but no

Deb. I looked to the left at the customer service desk thinking she might be talking to some of the women, but she wasn't there. *She'll be sorry she missed my grand entrance.*

Mike and Craig put me on the sofa in front of the fire. One of the women I remembered from this morning brought over a cup of hot chocolate. I grabbed onto it the best that I could, but my hands shook and I spilled some on my pants. It was so good to feel the warmth as it went down my throat, but boy, did I feel like an idiot. The kids that belonged to the family sitting around the fire stared at me like I was some kind of side show anomaly that they paid money to see. Note to self: don't stare at people who are hurt.

I was grateful for Mike and Craig. They didn't seem to care that people were staring; they must have been through this before. They tried to make me as comfortable as possible, but with movement came a horrid pain. I held my breath to prevent a moan from emanating from my lips, which was what I really wanted to do...if it hadn't been for all of my adoring fans gazing at me. I paid for the lack of pain I had on the mountain. Craig put his hand on the bottom of my boot and asked me to push. I couldn't put any pressure on his hand. He looked at Mike, so I looked at Mike waiting for a response. Nothing. Craig put his hand under my toes and told me to push one more time. I willed my toes to move, but I just couldn't get them to press against Craig's hand. He looked at Mike again, so I looked at Mike. Nothing. Another round of looks. Not being able to stand it anymore, I asked, "What's the verdict?"

Craig answered, "It looks like your leg is broken. It's not a compound fracture, though, so that's good. I just can't tell how much damage there is and where the break is in your leg."

Mike replied, "You need to get to the hospital—Crawford is the closest. We'll write directions for your wife. What kind of a car do you have?"

"A Jeep."

Mike said, "You'll have to sit in the back across the seat. No worry. We'll get you in."

This weekend was supposed to be a romantic interlude. Deb needed a break from all of the work she had been doing with the acting company, so I planned a ski trip. Not only did this vacation turn out to be a disaster, but now our lives would be anything but perfect for the next few months because of my dumb decision. As I daydreamed about how horrible this weekend turned out, one of the staff who Deb and I talked to earlier in the morning came over and asked me if I wanted anything to eat.

"No, thanks. I can't eat right now."

"Okay. Let me know if there is anything that I can do for you."

"Actually, you could do a favor for me."

Her eyes lit up. "Sure."

"My wife came to get help, but I haven't seen her. Have you?"

"No, sir, I haven't."

"Who took the information that I was hurt?"

"I did."

"What's your name?"

"Sarah."

"Sarah, thank you so much for sending out the help,"

and with a glimmer of hope I added, "I'm just wondering who reported my injury?"

"A guy who came across you on the trail."

"Did my wife come in at all?" Her confused look concerned me.

"I'm not sure. I'll ask the other people who are on duty."

"Thanks."

I rested my head on the back of the sofa and closed my eyes. Where was Deb?

Sarah came back and informed me, "No one has talked to or seen you wife. I remember her from this morning because she asked me if she should wear her heavy coat. Did she?"

"Yes, she did, but when I crashed into the tree, she gave it to me to sit on so I would stay warm."

"Now that's a woman. I'm going to look around. Maybe she's just trying to gather herself and hasn't realized how much time has passed."

"Thank you so much."

Craig said, "All we need is your wife so we can give her directions."

Craig and I sat in silence for a few minutes before Sarah approached me and said, "I haven't been able to find your wife. May I have your last name? I'll page her."

"Gallagher."

"I'll be right back."

I heard Deb paged to the front counter, and I looked all over the room hoping to see her walk around the corner. Nothing. No Deb.

I saw Sarah give a concerned look to Craig and Mike.

They got the hint and walked over to her. I wished I could hear what they were saying.

Where was she? All I could imagine was that she injured herself on one of the slopes. Or maybe she couldn't find her way back. Mike, Craig, and Sarah walked back to the sofa and stood over me.

I was the first one to speak. "We were lost and maybe she couldn't find her way back to the lodge."

"That's what we're thinking. We'll fire up the sled again and look for her."

"What does she look like?"

"She has brown, shoulder-length hair. She's wearing black ski pants and a red and black cross-country pullover that's not warm enough for this weather. She's been out there a long time."

"Don't worry; we'll go get her. We need you to relax, and we also need to get you to a hospital."

"I'm not going until I find Deb."

Mike was the first to answer. "Dan, we're going to find your wife, but we need you to be taken care of, too. We don't need two people to worry about."

Craig came back from outside and said, "Mike, Bruce is coming with me. Are you staying here?"

Mike said, "Yes."

"Okay, I'll keep you updated. There's another sled on its way from our downhill ski resort."

"Good." Then Mike asked, "Are they stopping here first?"

"Yes."

"I'll fill them in."

Bruce looked at Mike, "Take care."

Mike turned his attention back to me, "How are you feeling? Is the pain getting worse?"

"Yeah, it's getting worse."

"Well, I don't have any painkillers to give you. We're not permitted to medicate like that. If you want to get rid of the pain, the hospital is only twenty minutes away."

Panic rose deep in my chest. "I can't leave without my wife. Who knows what happened to her? I've been skiing a lot longer than she has and look what happened to me. And, she doesn't have her coat. I was going into hyperthermia and I had two coats. She only has a little thin pullover on. I can't believe this. I mean, she's still outside."

"Dan, I've worked with Bruce and Craig for years. They know these trails better than anyone else. They'll start with the trail you were on and branch out from there. Maybe your wife took another route, one that seemed more familiar to her."

Fear of what might have happened to Deb consumed me. "Yeah, and maybe she's lying somewhere freezing to death."

"We don't know that. I need you to think positive, and you need that, too. I'm going to tell you just a little bit about your injury because I need to focus on you right now. In EMT terms you are a class three right now, a broken bone. You could very easily slip to a class one, which is almost dead. I have no idea what is going on inside of your body. You need x-rays and the care of a doctor. You will be no good to your wife if you end up at a level one. And if you slip to a level one, that will cause us to pull our resources to take care of you. Is that what you want?"

"No. I want Deb found."

"The best way for us to do that is to get you out of here and to a hospital."

"I just can't leave her, though. What happens when she comes back here and I'm gone?"

"She'll be glad you're getting the care you need. You do need care, Dan, and you need it now. That pain isn't going to get any better without medication, and Dan, just so you know, if you pass out at any time, it's my job to give you the medical attention I see fit. The minute you close your eyes, I'll send for the ambulance."

It was a helpless feeling, and I knew I would feel guilty no matter what choice I made. I felt so selfish taking care of myself, but I knew Mike was right. I was taking away resources to find Deb. "If I go, will you please find my wife?"

Mike reassured me, "We'll find your wife, Dan."

I wanted all of this to just go away, but most of all I wanted Deb found so I said, "I trust you. I'll go to the hospital."

Mike requested an ambulance and knowing it was on its way had me feeling like I was abandoning Deb. All that time I spent on the mountain wondering why it was taking so long, and Deb was lost after all. I just thank God that the skier not only came by, but also that he didn't listen to me when I told him help was on its way. If he hadn't reported my accident, then both Deb and I would be in worse shape now. I could at least feel comforted by that knowledge.

Mike consoled me, "Dan, like I promised you, we'll find your wife. I'm on my way out now to look for her, but you will be in good hands. The EMTs are excellent and Crawford Hospital has great doctors."

"Thanks, Mike."

"You're doing the right thing."

"I know you're right, it is just so hard to leave."

"I can only imagine how you must feel, but we'll take care of everything."

"Mike, what do you think happened to my wife?"

"I think she must have gotten turned around somehow. She's probably on the far end of the mountain away from the lodge. You said that the two of you were lost in the first place, so getting acclimated with the area, especially after witnessing an accident like yours, can be very difficult."

"Will you bring her to the hospital?"

"We'll get her to you."

"I'd appreciate that. Thank you for all of your help."

"You're welcome."

Mike put his hand on my shoulder and disappeared out the door as the ambulance crew arrived. Mike said something to them, and they all turned and looked my way. I'm sure he told them of my injuries; I just didn't like the look of pity that came over their faces a few seconds later when he told them about Deb.

———

The new EMTs introduced themselves to me. "Hi, Dan. My name is Brian and this is my partner, Matt. We hear you're not doing so well. We'll get you taken care of."

"Thanks." I made one more attempt. "I guess I can't stay and wait for my wife?"

Brian replied, "Mike told us about your wife, and I know they are working very hard to find her. I'd love to say 'yes' but that isn't possible. If you refuse treatment and we get another call, we'll have to leave you here. You would be looking at several hours before we could return. And there isn't a guarantee that another ambulance would be close by."

Brian and Matt did their best to help me get over my guilt for leaving. "Dan, we don't understand exactly how you're feeling, but we do understand that this must be difficult. If you would reverse the roles, say Deb was here with a broken leg and you were still out on the mountain, would you want her to seek medical attention?"

"Of course."

"You wouldn't want her to feel guilty and ashamed for leaving."

"No."

"I think your wife would feel the same way."

"Yes, she would want me to go."

"Okay. We'll go get the stretcher and carry you out to the ambulance."

Once in the ambulance, I considered the irony of this being my second first ride of the day. First the snowmobile and now the ambulance. I liked the snowmobile better. Brian remained in the back with me while Matt drove. Brian asked, "How are you doing so far? Are you warm enough?"

"Yes, I'm warm, but my leg is really starting to bother me."

"Once we get to the hospital, you'll be examined and you'll have x-rays taken. After that, the doctor will give you some painkillers."

I closed my eyes and recalled the events that led up to my accident. First we started out in the lodge. Deb didn't know whether or not to wear her heavy ski coat. As I looked around for goggles, Deb walked up to the counter and asked one of the staff members, Sarah, if she should take the extra coat. Later when we were on the mountain Deb told me that Sarah said it's better to be too warm than too cold. We left the lodge, skied around the back, and then I remembered actually looking at the snowmobile that ended up rescuing me. I also remembered wondering when they had last used it.

We then chose to take the trail that runs below the Mount Washington Hotel. Part of the trail crossed a golf course, and skiing through that flat, open area was brutal with the wind. Deb and I talked about the cold weather and that there weren't as many people out skiing. As we got into the woods, the wind wasn't as bad, and we did feel warmer. Deb asked me how long it would take to get to the tent. I wasn't sure, but I did know that we would get in a good run before we got to it. We were both looking forward to the day, to getting to the tent, and then to taking a nap or sitting by the fire back at the lodge. After Deb asked about the directions to the tent, she said, "Dan, I think I drank too much coffee at breakfast because I really have to go to the bathroom." I told her to find a good, secluded spot. I was her lookout. Whenever we were in the woods and Deb had to go to the bathroom, she continually asked, "Is it still okay? Is anybody coming?" I always asked her why she even bothered to have me as the lookout because I would certainly tell her if someone were approaching. It was just after that we ran into that crazy mountain man.

The mountain man. I didn't think about that guy until now. I didn't like what I could see in his eyes. He stared at Deb as he went past us. I'm not a jealous guy. Plenty of guys look at Deb; she's beautiful. The problem with this man was the way he looked at her; it was strange. We were on a hill; he was skiing down, and we had just started up. After a few steps, this guy should have been out of our sight. I turned around to look for him, and he had stopped in the middle of the trail and was looking up at us. At first I thought he might be resting, but because I felt uneasy about him I watched him closely. He didn't even flinch or seem embarrassed that I caught him looking at my wife. He stood his ground, but I stood mine. After a few seconds of staring, I said, "Can I help you? Stare at someone else." Then I started toward him, but he turned and skied away. After I broke my leg, I forgot about this incident. Even when I was on the mountain with time to think, it wasn't on my mind, but now that Deb was missing, I remembered it clearly. I opened my eyes and said to Brian, "I think someone may have taken my wife."

Chapter 4

All the world's a stage,
And all the men and women merely players;
They have their exits and their entrances...
                    —William Shakespeare

Here I was sitting in the front row of a theater with the lights on full blast. The only thing that would have made this event even more pathetic is if I had a spotlight shining right on my face with a banner hanging above my head that said *Dan Gallagher is here. He is right here.* (Big flashing neon arrow would be pointing at me). *He tricked Nancy into letting him chaperone this play so that he could see you again. He's not totally pathetic or anything. Oh, and he also isn't stalking you. He just really liked you that day in the parking lot and this is the best plan he could come up with to get a date with you.*

But seeing Deb's sparkling blue eyes and bright smile melted away all of my nerves. She made eye contact with the audience and as she spied me, her smile grew even bigger. Nancy leaned forward at the other end of the aisle and mouthed, "So she's the reason!" *Just take me now, God.*

While strolling to the end of the stage, Deb said, "I see lots of attentive, intelligent students here with their attentive and intelligent teachers. We have such a treat for you. 'The Tell-Tale Heart' by Edgar Allan Poe. If you thought it was scary reading it, just wait until you see it performed."

We really didn't need to see "The Tell-Tale Heart" performed because I was sure everyone around me could hear my heart beating just fine. My heart kept telling me this is one talented, attractive, adorable woman.

Deb continued to introduce each story to be performed, "'Guy de Maupassant's 'The Monkey's Paw.' You will all experience the adage 'be careful what you wish for.'"

Okay, I wish Deb would come down from the stage, wrap her arms around me, and put her full, soft lips to mine. Hmmmm, she was still on stage. Maybe I needed the monkey's paw for it to work.

Deb addressed the crowd, "We have a special treat for you today. After the show, you are all welcome to stay for a short question-and-answer session. For those of you who have a bit of driving to do, we understand, and we'll give you a few minutes to exit."

Nancy leaned forward again and gave me a nod and a thumbs up. I guess that meant we were staying.

Deb played the lead in "The Necklace," and she did a convincing job of making the audience feel her pain of having lost her friend's diamond necklace, and then working her whole life to pay it back only to find out what she thought were diamonds were really paste. Next, the troupe adapted one of Twain's tales; Deb acted in this story, too, delivering her lines with expert comedic timing. The audience loved her, and I could feel myself falling in love with her, too. The students were, as Deb said, attentive. They seemed to have had a good time and showed their appreciation with their applause. As the curtain closed, the house lights came up, and Deb and the rest of the actors appeared on stage.

Deb said, "We'll take as many questions as we can. Who would like to start?"

Part of me wanted to raise my hand, but a student from another school beat me to it. He must have been all of fifteen. He asked, "How did you all get started in this business?"

There were various answers from each of the actors, but I really anticipated Deb's response. "Well, I love acting. I started when I was in high school, just like all of you. In tenth grade I tried out for the musical. I made it, and I loved it so much that I tried out for summer theater that year. I enjoy being in this company because I enjoy traveling and I enjoy literature."

As I looked around at Deb's fellow actors, it struck me just how good looking these men were. I wondered if she was seeing any of them.

Nancy kept looking back and forth between Deb and me. Nancy must have read my mind because she raised her hand and asked, "Do any of you have families, and if so, how do you handle being away so much?" She's good. I was secretly glad she was sharing my room this year.

Again, various answers from the cast. Most were single and when it came time for Deb to answer I held my breath.

"I'm single, so the traveling really isn't a problem."

That made every minute leading up to this trip worth it.

The cast graciously took several more questions, and then they thanked us for coming. They mingled with us, shaking our hands as we left. Deb approached me and I couldn't take my eyes off her. There was an energy about her that I found appealing. Deb put her soft hand in mine, but I felt something rough on her palm. A piece of paper. When she pulled her hand away, I grasped the paper in my fist hoping no one saw it. I was the happiest man on earth, and I didn't even know what was written on the paper. It could be "stop stalking me," but I wouldn't care after watching her graceful figure glide toward me, never taking her blue eyes off mine. I would die a happy man if that was the only memory I ever had of her.

Time to go. Nancy ushered the students to the back of the theater and into the lobby. I brought up the end of the line so I could spend more time around Deb. I felt like if I went, that's it. I wouldn't see her again. The cast waved as the last of us exited. I was elated and nervous at the same time, but my nerves seemed to have won out in that little contest as my damp hands moistened the piece of paper. Once on the bus, Nancy counted the students and then told the bus driver to head back to school. Nancy sat next to me and asked, "Well, what did she hand to you?"

I opened my fist. Looking at the paper, Nancy clapped. "What does it say?"

Here goes. "I couldn't believe that my knight in shining armor was here. I hope you liked the play. I'm glad you came. I'll be in town tonight, but I'm leaving in the morning for Dallas. If you can, call me."

"She gave me her phone number and asked me to call her tonight."

"Yes, Roomie, we did it! This totally paid off. I'm so happy for you. You are going to call her."

"Yes, I'll call her later today."

"Good. This is so exciting. To think, I might have been witness to the blossoming of my Roomie's new romance."

Nancy smiled the whole bus ride back to school. I must admit, I was excited, too. Once the students exited the bus Nancy said, "I hope everything works out tonight. You don't have to tell me what happens, especially if it doesn't work out. Well, unless you want to tell me. That would be just fine."

"Thanks, Nancy. Here's the deal. If things work out, I'll tell you. If they don't, we'll just pretend that none of this ever happened."

"I'm glad she was there. Oh, if you want some advice, tell her that she had great stage presence. I dabble in the theater here at school, so from my experience, I think she would like hearing a compliment like that. Have a great evening."

———◆———

I brought some papers home to grade. More of a distraction, really. I kept looking at the equations, making sure all of the work led to the correct answer. One student, Scott, amazingly had all of the right answers without having done any of the work. I have a plan in such cases. Tomorrow, as I hand back all of the papers, Scott's won't be among them. When he comes up to me and says, "Mr. Gallagher you didn't hand back my paper," then I'll ask, "How did you come up with all of the right answers without doing any of the work?" Scott will stand in front of me for a second trying to come up with a response, and when he can't, I'll give Scott a different worksheet, created for such cases, and let him do his own work for half credit. We will also have the "when you copy someone else's work, you're only cheating yourself" talk.

I knew I was avoiding the issue. I removed Deb's phone number from my pocket and without thinking about it anymore, I dialed.

One ring, two rings, three rings. I was about to hang up when there was a voice at the other end, "Hello."

"Hello," I said as I was interrupted by, "I can't come to the phone right now..." but then the message was cut off by, "Hello, hi, I'm here. Just let me turn this thing off. Okay."

"Hi, Deb, it's Dan."

"Dan, I was hoping you would call. Sorry about the machine. I just got out of the shower. I was trying to get all of this makeup off from this afternoon's performance."

"Your acting company sure knows how to entertain high school students. They talked about it the whole way back to the school. You were terrific by the way." Now what was it I was supposed to say? Oh yeah. I added, "I like your stage presence."

"Thanks, no one's ever said that to me before."

Score one for me. "Well, someone should have because it's true."

"That's very nice of you, Dan. Did you have a good time this afternoon?"

"I did. It was my first school trip to a play."

"I'm sure it was. You teach science, right?"

"Physics. Our field trips consist of egg drops off the roof of the school, pedometer measurements in the parking lot, that sort of thing. It was a treat to break out of the routine."

"How did you get to go since the play didn't exactly

relate to your subject? It's not like we did a performance about Einstein."

"Well, in our overcrowded school, all of the teachers have to share rooms. I happen to share mine with an English teacher. She needed another chaperone for this field trip, so I went along." *I leave out the part where I orchestrated the whole thing.*

"So you are a knight in shining armor rescuing young maidens."

"Something like that."

I stalled for time, trying to decide if I should ask Deb out for dinner or just coffee. I didn't want to look cheap.

"Have you had dinner yet?"

"Yes, I ate after the performance. I was starving. Did you eat?"

"Yes. I usually have an early dinner. Would you like to meet for coffee?"

"That would be great, I'd love to."

"I know you are new to the area. Have you heard of Stoudt's Restaurant?"

"Yes. It's actually right up the street from me. It is one of the few places I know around here."

"When can you be ready?"

"Half an hour."

"Half an hour it is. I'll see you then, Deb."

"I'm looking forward to it, Dan."

———◆———

This whole plan actually worked out. Nancy will be thrilled to hear this.

What to wear? I didn't want to show up with what I had on for school today. I needed something a little more casual. I stood in front of my closet trying to figure that out. One casual Friday I wore a pair of dark-wash jeans and a black turtleneck sweater to school. When Nancy walked into my room, she went crazy for the outfit. She said that I looked hip. Nancy has good taste, so I'll wear that. I had just enough time to take a quick shower, spray on some Hugo Boss cologne, and run a comb through my hair before running out the door.

Stoudt's is a nice family restaurant. They've been in business for a long time; they have great food and even better pies. I was first to arrive, but I wanted it that way. The waitress put me at a booth by some windows. About five minutes later a car pulled into the parking lot. Deb got out of a small black car. She wore tight jeans tucked into black leather boots and a black turtleneck sweater. If she weren't so much better looking than me, I would say we looked like twins.

The hostess brought Deb to the booth and I slid out and stood until she was seated.

"Hi, you look stunning."

"Hey, how are you since we last spoke?"

"I was good before, but I'm great now."

"Oh, why is that?"

"Because I'm here with you."

"Thank you. I feel the same way."

"Have you ordered yet?"

"Absolutely not."

"Good, what would you suggest?"

"A cup of coffee; they brew a mean cup. And their pies are delicious. Coconut custard is my favorite."

"Coffee and pie it is."

Our waitress was a young girl. "How are yoose tonight?"

Nancy must be rubbing off on me because the sound of that word goes through me. I never thought that incorrect English would bother me. I am, after all, one of the biggest culprits of butchering the English language, or so I'm told by our Language Arts staff.

"We're just fine," I answered, "and how are you?" *Emphasis on the you without the "s."*

My attempt went unnoticed. "Great, could I start yoose off with something to drink?"

I turned to Deb, "Do you know what you want?"

"I sure do. I'll have a cup of coffee and a slice of coconut custard pie."

"I'll have the same."

The waitress said, "Thanks, I'll be right back with your coffee."

I wanted to know all about Deb, but I contained myself and just asked, "What is your next adventure with the theater company?"

"Tomorrow we leave for Dallas. We'll be there for three days, and then we're off to Missouri for another three days. Then we'll be in Chicago about a week. We have off for a few weeks for Christmas. They arrange it that way because the actors need a break to see their families, and the kids are off from school anyway. I don't know how many students would want to give up part of their break to see a play."

"I don't know. Some of our teachers take students on field trips over weekends and over part of the summer. The trips are always booked and everyone has a good time. It's kind of hard to explain if you haven't taken kids on a trip. It's a different experience to see students in a whole other learning environment. I was surprised how many thank you notes I received from parents appreciating the time I took for the trip. It ends up meaning a great deal to everyone."

"I remember my high school English teacher taking our class to see *Hamlet* at Princeton University. I was so excited I can't even begin to tell you. I dressed in a nice skirt and sweater and completed the ensemble with a pair of pearls because I thought they made me look older. I don't know what I was thinking. Maybe that some college guy would be interested. How stupid, really. The big, yellow school bus had to be a total turn off. That and our teacher yelling, 'This way, class.' And I don't think my paper bag lunch was a man magnet either."

I laughed at that. "I can relate. It makes me think that I must embarrass some of my students when I take them on trips."

"No. I bet your students love you. You seemed at ease with them at the play and they really seem to like you."

"That's nice of you to say."

Deb added, "What are some field trips you've taken your class on?"

"Physics doesn't allow for that many places to visit. I do take my class to a sort of Science Olympics. And we usually go to a few college science fairs. To tell you the truth, seeing your play today was a nice change of pace from $E=mc^2$. I enjoyed not only the performance but also the kids enjoying the performance."

"You enjoyed it?"

"Yes, I told you I did."

Deb laughed, "I like to hear it, though. We don't get much feedback because we are never in one place for long. Even though we're in Chicago for a week, we'll be at a different location each day."

"Does that kind of life take a toll on you?"

"No, not really. My friends are part of the troupe and I love seeing the country. I get paid to do it, too."

"What was your favorite place to visit?"

"On the play tour or on vacation?"

"Either."

"Let's see. I really enjoyed Santa Fe, New Mexico. Old Town is beautiful. There are shops, art galleries, and other interesting places to see. Santa Fe was the last leg of one of our tours and I decided to stay on for a few more days. Did you ever hear of the mystery of the wooden staircase that uses no nails?"

"No, I never heard of it. Did you see it?"

"Yes, I did. It's in a church. The stairs are amazing and very steep. I wouldn't want to climb them. Originally there was no railing, but the nuns used it so often that a carpenter put a railing on it."

"What's the mystery?"

"I don't remember all of the details of the story, but it's something about a carpenter appearing from nowhere, building the staircase for the nuns, and then disappearing, never to be heard from again. I guess I should look it up sometime to refresh my memory. Have you ever been to New Mexico?"

"No, I've been to Montana and Arizona, but that's it for out west."

Deb asked which one I liked better.

"Montana. I felt at home there when I finally visited, but it has been calling me ever since sixth grade."

"Really? How?"

"I just remember thinking about Montana all of the time, wondering what it would be like. In my mind I created my own Montana, complete with cowboys, which might be why I thought I heard it calling me. I always wanted to be a cowboy; I like their lifestyle of sleeping under the stars at night and riding across the land during the day. Kind of a romantic image, I know. I left out the rain, snow, and cold; in my dreams every day was perfect weather."

"So what did you like about it?"

"How open it is. How majestic it is. How relaxed it is."

"When did you go?"

"I went five years ago. My buddy Mark is an outdoor guy and we went together. I wanted to see Glacier National Park before all of the glaciers disappeared. I was watching a show about the national parks one evening, and the report on Glacier said that they would be gone in about thirty years. That's why we went, to make sure we saw them. "

Deb was easy to talk to. I could see the two of us years from now sitting on our front porch reminiscing, feeling content and just as comfortable.

The waitress interrupted my trip into the future to check on us. "How is everything here?"

"Deb, would you like another cup of coffee or anything?"

"No thanks. I'll be up all night if I have another cup. I'm fine."

I turned to the waitress with regret knowing the evening was coming to a close. "Nothing for me either. I'll just take the check."

Deb tilted her head and said, "Thanks. This was really nice. It's hard for me to meet people, and I don't want to hang out with the actors from the troupe all of the time. I see them enough."

"It was my pleasure." I paid the bill, and Deb and I walked to the parking lot together.

I wanted to see Deb again. I organized this whole scenario; I didn't want it to end now. I asked, "Can I call you?"

"That would be wonderful! My schedule is crazy, though, for the next few weeks. Why don't you call me when I get back from Chicago? I would love to see you again."

"Great, I'll call you in a couple of weeks."

Deb hesitated for a second, and then leaned in and gave me a kiss on the lips, "Good night, *good knight!*"

The softness of her lips on mine and her perfume still in the air, I was ready to scale any castle wall or slay any dragon. I found myself wishing away the next few weeks.

———————

The next day at school, as Nancy promised, she didn't say a thing about whether or not I called Deb. She did exclaim, "Hi, Roomie," like she usually does when I walk in the room. I responded with "Good morning," and that was it. I wanted to tell her about yesterday, but I also wanted to play it cool. I put my bag down, and while I gathered my papers and plan book I told Nancy, "Well, I called Deb last night."

"Good for you! And…"

"We met for coffee."

"Where did you go?"

"Stoudt's."

Nancy responded, "How was it?'

"Good. I had the coconut custard pie."

Nancy rolled her eyes, "No, I mean your date."

I laughed. "I know. Deb and I talked for a long time, and I felt comfortable with her. I think she felt comfortable with me, too."

"Awesome. And to think I was witness to the blooming of what could be a beautiful love story."

"Yes, you said that on the bus. Don't push it. I'm supposed to call her when she gets back to town in a few weeks, but that's it."

"But that's good. So, she said for you to call her or is she calling you?"

"I'm going to call her."

"I'm happy for you. Do you like this Deb?"

"Yes, I do."

"Yippee, my Roomie's in love! Can I come to the wedding?"

"Nancy, that looks like an awful big pile of papers to grade."

Then it was Nancy's turn to laugh, "I get the hint. Don't worry, Roomie, your secret is safe with me."

Chapter 5

If the eye does not want to see, neither light
nor glasses will help.
— German Proverb

Brian repeated my words, "What do you mean 'someone may have taken your wife?'"

"We were skiing and a guy came past us and kept watching Deb. I noticed him because he made such a point of staring at us. And I'm not being paranoid either. I must have forgotten about him, but now that Deb is missing, this guy has me concerned."

"I'll inform the rescue squad back at the resort."

Brian opened the window to the driver and revealed my theory. I could hear Matt radio the resort. I didn't like the look in Brian's eyes, although I couldn't tell if it was because he looked like he thought I was a lunatic or if it was because he believed me. *When will this nightmare be over?* I couldn't even help Deb. All I could do was just lie on the stretcher with my eyes closed, wishing I could start the day over again.

Brian interrupted my thoughts. "Dan, how long have you been a cross-country skier?"

"About twenty years."

"I've been skiing about the same amount of time.

Growing up in New Hampshire, the only two choices I had were downhill or cross-country skiing. I tried both, but I really enjoyed the solitude of being in the back country, so my choice was made. All this time I've never run into anyone shady; cross-country skiing is just too much work for a criminal. Don't you agree?"

"Yeah, putting it that way, it makes sense. I've never felt uncomfortable about anyone I've come across on the trails."

"Maybe that's what you need to concentrate on."

"Until today." I knew I couldn't let him change my mind. If I did and this creep had Deb, then the police might ignore that as a possibility. Brian stopped talking. I knew he was trying to make me feel better, but nothing would do that until Deb was found safe.

We pulled up to the hospital, and Brian and Matt grabbed a wheelchair from the security guard at the door. *A security guard at the front entrance of this little hospital in this little town?* Inside the hospital was a greeting party, The Women's Club. Nice little old ladies with coffee and homemade cookies. When Brian and Matt wheeled me through the lobby, I found out that the refreshments were not for me or any other patient; they're for the visitors.

Matt and Brian maneuvered me over to the receptionist's desk, and she asked me for my insurance card. *My wife is missing and I'm being asked for my insurance card?* This was all surreal. When I didn't respond, the receptionist tried again, "Sir, your insurance card? Sir, are you all right?"

Are you kidding? No, I'm not all right. Brian must have seen the look on my face because he answered, "Emily."

They must be on a first name basis here. I wondered how

many times a week these guys end up here. Probably quite a few for downhill skiers. I was probably the first idiot to break his leg cross-country skiing.

Brian continued, "Dan, is your wallet in your backpack?"

Matt held my backpack while Brian looked for my wallet. He found it and gave the receptionist all the cards she needed to take down my information. I was certain that I was in a dream or maybe watching a movie. *All of this must be happening to someone else.* I closed my eyes hoping that the next time I opened them I would be at home in the morning with Deb lying beside me still asleep. I let my mind take me back to that place where I turn over and I tell Deb I love her. She wakes up and draws herself a bubble bath while I stay in bed thinking about my lovely wife just on the other side of the door, her body glistening and wet with the bubbles highlighting all of my favorite parts. I throw the covers off, open the door, and Deb says, "I knew you couldn't resist," and as I step in the warm water beside my wife, I say, "I never could." Once we are rested, we'll take a drive through the country and stop for ice cream at a little roadside stand. She'll order mint chocolate chip in a sugar cone, and I'll get a regular cone of rocky road. *Rocky road.* What irony. That doesn't even come close to describing this day.

"Sir, we're going to lift you up here so that we can take an x-ray of your leg."

All I wanted was to stay in that memory with Deb, but I had to snap out of it. I wasn't sure if I felt helpless, guilty, enraged, self-pity, or all of them combined. Whatever it was, it was ugly, and I needed to get out of it if I was going to help Deb. Once I regained my senses and started to think clearly, I remembered there was someone who could help me. My brother-in-law, Joel, is a police detective, and I knew he could get me the help I needed. Back in my room, I asked for the cellphone that was in my backpack. It rang three times on the other end before Joel picked up.

"Joel, it's Dan."

"Hey, buddy. How are you?"

"I've been better. Listen, I need some help."

"What's wrong? You don't sound like yourself."

"I'm not." Maybe it was talking to someone familiar. Maybe it was the urgency I heard in Joel's voice, but finally my breaking point arrived. Through tears I told my brother-in-law the whole story, and with each detail I revealed, the words that echoed back to me sounded crazy and tragic, and I sensed that if this were a movie, there would be no possibility of a happy ending.

Chapter 6

All through the year
We've waited
Waited through spring and fall
To hear silver bells ringing
See winter time bringing
The happiest season of all.
— The Carpenters

The weeks after the play were a blur. That always happens, though, around Christmas break. The realization that I don't have as much time as I thought to cover all of the curriculum sets in. Now I needed to decide how I was going to cram in two units before the middle of January, the semester end. I had a lot to keep my mind focused on other than Deb and the phone call, but I still found my mind always going back to her no matter what else I had going on. I thought about what would happen when Deb was back in town. I also wondered about the connection I felt to her. This had never happened to me before. I spent the first few years of my twenties playing basketball, having Texas-hold-'em tournaments, and golfing with my buddies. One great thing about my friends is that we all have the same interests, so there was always something for us to do. As time went on, most of them met the woman of their dreams and got married. That meant fewer and fewer outings for them. Once in a while we all get together and have a blast, but the dynamics have changed. Mark and I were the only ones living the bachelor life well into our late twenties. Mark still doesn't want to settle down, but I was afraid I would be the only one left sponsoring a solitaire tournament. Mark is happy moving from one woman to the next, and women just love him, too. I don't get it. What attracts women to a man who has no interest in them other than bed? I'm ready to settle down. I didn't feel this way in my twenties, and I had plenty of women who would have been happy to join me in marital bliss.

———————

I woke up on the morning of December twenty-third to the sound of rain on the roof. Why couldn't it be snow? It was the last school day of the year. Yesterday, I gave a test to end the unit on acceleration. My plans for the day included homemade paper car races. It might not sound like it, but it's very exciting, well, to me at least. This is one of the toughest days of the school year. Students don't want to work, and there are no holiday festivities planned. The students spend most of the day asking why nothing has been planned, and then they ask every teacher that day if they can go around the school caroling or see if anybody is having parties. Parties are frowned upon; every day is supposed to be a learning day, but I have noticed that adding a bowl of popcorn to the classroom makes even a huge test feel like a party.

The paper car races will keep my students occupied, and they will be able to apply the principles of acceleration. Like most of my colleagues, I won't be giving notes because I know that information won't sink in, and ten days is too long for me to expect the class to remember new information. I'll just end up re-teaching the same thing on the first day back in January.

I carefully chose my outfit for today last night: my favorite black pants with a red shirt that I only wear once a year. The tie is black with candy canes on it. The number of compliments I receive when I wear this is staggering.

It was still raining as I walked to my car, but not as hard. Just a light drizzle, and just enough to be annoying on a cold day. I'll take rain over ice, but I really wished this were snow, only if we had a snow day, though. I don't like thinking about students who just received their licenses driving in that kind of weather.

The school parking lot was much emptier than usual. Seemed everyone was taking their time today. Maybe they were just hoping the rain would turn to snow. They're out of luck, though—no snow day today. I like getting to school before the chaos sets in. Some teachers walk in with the students, but I enjoy the extra half an hour of serenity. Okay, so I do have Nancy in my room and I have that whole "Good morning, Roomie" thing to deal with, but there is something I love about the empty hallways in the morning. I think it's the anticipation of the day, looking forward to sharing my knowledge with students. I love to see their progress throughout the year and being in the empty hallways reminds me of what's missing, and why I'm here.

As I approached my door, I could see the light was already on. Nancy. She must sleep here. I only had one foot in the door when she exclaimed, "Merry Christmas-Eve eve, Roomie!"

"That's original, Nancy. You English teachers just amaze me with your creativity."

"Yeah, well, that's just about as original as that tie. Didn't you wear that last Christmas-Eve eve?"

"Your charm holds no bounds."

"Thanks, Roomie! Hey, I love the tie. I probably told you that last year, though."

"Nancy, whose room are you sharing next semester?"

"Well, I was saving this for your Christmas gift, but *yours*, Roomie. You get me again next semester."

"Gee, there really is a Santa Claus."

"I knew you'd be happy."

"Honestly, Nancy. I'm glad that you're in my room. I haven't had to worry about the gas jets being turned on, or my room being left a disaster. And, you helped me with Deb."

"Tonight's the night, isn't it?"

"If you mean she's back in town and I'm calling her, then you're right."

"Good luck. I shouldn't have said that. I hate saying 'good luck' to people. Have you ever read *The Catcher in the Rye?*"

"No."

"The main character hates saying good luck to people because he feels it's condescending, that luck is the only thing that will help. Not intellect, savvy or anything else. So forget I said 'good luck.' Instead, I hope it goes well and that whatever happens is what is best for you."

"Thanks, Nancy."

"And just like before, I won't ask how it went."

I grinned. "It's going to go very well. I'm Dan Gallagher, after all," and then I added, "I am grateful for all you have done for me, Nancy. Of course I'll tell you what happens. It's the least I can do for my..." *God, help me for calling her this,* "Roomie."

The noise in the hallway grew louder and louder so I ended the conversation. "Nancy, I hope you have a good day, and if I don't see you before the end of school, have a very Merry Christmas!"

Then the fire alarm went off.

———•◦•———

Of all days for a fire alarm. It was raining outside, and how in the world were we going to get students interested in learning after this? I stuck my head in the hallway and smelled smoke. This obviously wasn't a drill and this wasn't going to be a quick in-and-out-of-the-building, so I grabbed my coat and headed out the door.

The entire school, staff and students, filed into the parking lot behind the school. The mist coming down was irritating; it was the kind of fine rain that stays on top of hair and coat and doesn't seem wet until you run your hand over the surface and find it's soaked. The roar of the fire engines grew closer, so we ushered the kids who were standing in the road back behind the parked cars. There was a lot of complaining coming out of the kids. Statements like, "This is a great last day." "Yeah, it sure is." "First they don't let us have any parties, and now they're making us stand in the rain." "Maybe they'll let us go home now!" And then there's always the optimist, "Maybe the school will burn down."

As the fire engines stopped behind the building and the firemen piled out, the principal met them at the door. I looked up to my left and saw Nancy walking over to me without her coat, shivering. As she stood next to me, I took my coat off and wrapped it around her shoulders. She looked at me and said, "You're a lifesaver. It is so cold out here." A few minutes later the assistant principal appeared from inside the lower set of doors and summoned the teachers. Nancy and I arrived first. "Someone started a fire in a trash can in the boys' bathroom on the second floor. We need to separate the student body and keep them confined to one area until the investigation is complete." This day just kept getting better and better by the minute. At least we were going to be out of this rain and inside, but we were going to be inside with half of the students. Tough call. The assistant principal continued, "I want you to make sure these students all go to the auditorium. Block entrances to the other hallways and stairwells. No one is to go anywhere else in this building."

I replied, "No problem. We'll get it done." Then we motioned for the students to come inside. One of the math teachers was manning the door and instructing the students to proceed to the auditorium. There was a lot of mumbling and grumbling, but also a lot of excitement for not having to go to class. The teachers who were in the upper part of the parking lot had to take their students to the gymnasium. I was glad we would have comfortable seats with cushions to sit on instead of the hard bleachers in the gym.

So there we were in a holding pattern in the auditorium until the principal caught the perpetrator, and suddenly the spirit of the season came over the group. As the house lights dimmed, the stage lights came up, and microphones were turned on. One of the senior choir girls began singing a beautiful rendition of Karen Carpenter's "Merry Christmas, Darling." Nancy walked from the back of the auditorium and sat next to me, still wearing my coat. The song brought back wonderful memories of Christmas past spending the morning around the tree with my mom and dad and sister. The song ended and in the dark I felt Nancy's hand on my knee as she stood up and put my coat over my lap. Leaning over she said, "Wait till you hear this one, Roomie." Nancy ran down the aisle and up the stairs to the stage and sang, "All I Want For Christmas is You." The audience was mesmerized by Nancy's voice, and even after working with her for so many years, it was a side of her that I had never seen. As Nancy finished the song, the spotlight illuminated her face as she looked my way and winked. The smile that came over my face was interrupted by the voice from the intercom for all of us to return to our classrooms.

The teachers sprang to attention and ushered the students out of the auditorium. I wished it could have lasted a little longer. On my way out I called to Nancy over the murmuring voices of the students, "Nancy."

She turned around and I put my hand up for a high-five and said, "Now, that's real stage presence."

Nancy stopped for a second and studied me before returning my high-five and said, "Hey, are you finished with your Christmas shopping?"

"I still need to get something for Deb. I was thinking of running to Tiffany's."

"Tiffany's? Wow. Just remember, Roomie, be careful what you do in the beginning of the relationship because you'll be expected to do it for the rest of the relationship."

"That's great advice, Nancy."

"I learned that the hard way."

"I won't ask."

"Good, because I wouldn't tell you anyway."

———

I looked forward to the end of the school day. I'd never been in Tiffany's before, but I was sure I would find something nice. Oh, yes, the fire. Well, all of that got sorted out. Here's the story: A girl decided to set a fire in the trash can in the boys' bathroom. I'm not sure why she started it, but using the boys' bathroom as a decoy was brilliant. Everybody was looking at the guys, but it was a girl. I don't know this particular young lady so I wondered if she used this craftiness when completing her assignments for school. Somehow I doubted it.

When the last bell of the day rang, sounds of "Have a great vacation," "Merry Christmas," "Happy Holidays," and the very popular, "See you next year," filled the bustling hallways. Nancy filed into my room and started packing her bag.

"Wow, Nancy, what is all of that you have?"

"Presents."

"Presents from whom?"

"Students."

"What did you get?"

Nancy rifled through her bag and pulled out the gifts one by one. "First, I was given Godiva chocolates."

"That's a huge box. Are you sure you can eat all of that chocolate yourself? If you need some help, I would be happy to oblige."

"It's a long break, Dan. I'm sure I can manage. Next is an array of lotions from Bath and Body Works."

"I think the kids are trying to tell you something."

"Jealousy is not an attractive attribute, Dan. I was also given a crystal Christmas ornament, a book, and a box of homemade cookies. I'm so blessed. What did you get?"

"Well, let me just dig in my bag of goodies, and see what I pull out first. Oh, here, a candy cane."

"That's sweet. What else?"

"Uh, this candy cane." Nancy started laughing.

"Look, I can't help that you're a freak of nature. Secondary teachers aren't supposed to get gifts. That job's reserved for teachers of little kids."

"It's okay, Dan. Maybe someday you can be like me. Would you like a chocolate?"

"I'd love one!" She handed me her box of Godiva chocolates, and I picked out a little one that looked like it might contain caramel. Luck was on my side. Creamy caramel. "Delicious. Are you going to use all of that lotion? The raspberry you have there is my favorite."

"Ha, ha."

"See, Nancy, everyone likes you around here. No one else got an armload of gifts like that."

"Do you have everything packed up to go home?"

"Well, there isn't much to pack, but yeah, I'm ready."

Changing the subject, Nancy asked, "Are you still making a stop at Tiffany's?"

"It's only the twenty-third of December so I don't think that the King of Prussia Mall will be that crowded at three thirty. I should get down there by that time if I leave now."

"Oh, you poor boy. You don't go shopping very often, do you?"

"No, especially not at King of Prussia!"

"Do you even know where Tiffany's is?"

"Good point. No, I don't."

"Okay, it's in the part with Nordstrom and Neiman Marcus. Don't go in the Bloomingdale's part of the mall, you'll be on the wrong side."

"So I'm to go in on the Bloomin' Marcus side, not the Nordstromdale's side."

"You can't be that dumb."

"Actually, Nancy, I could be, but thankfully I'm not. I will head for the Neiman Marcus side of the mall. That's an expensive store isn't it?"

"You're hopeless. So you're still on the Tiffany's kick?"

"It's not a kick. It's the right thing to do."

"What is Deb getting you? I mean what if she gives you, oh, I don't know, a cupcake for instance?"

"I'll enjoy every last crumb!"

"Well, I hope she gives you more than a cupcake."

"Material things are not important to me. I'll just be happy to spend some time with her."

"And on that note, I do hope you have a Merry Christmas and a Happy New Year!"

"You too, Nancy."

Nancy left first and when I finally made it out to the parking lot, she was still packing her car with all of the gifts. I drove past and waved thinking to myself, "See, Dan, there is a good thing about not getting all of those presents!"

The drive down to King of Prussia is not one of my favorites. Nancy was right when she said that I wasn't a shopper. I don't know my way around this mall. It's huge. It's actually two malls joined by a little, okay, a long walkway, and the colder the weather, the longer the walkway becomes.

And I was wrong about the three-thirty thing. The parking lot was packed. It's nuts. People in cars were following other people walking out of the mall and asking, "Are you leaving?" How stupid. Why would anyone do that? They should just drive around until they find a parking space. It can't be that hard. After a few trips around both malls and over each level of the parking garages, I glanced at the clock on my dash and it read three fifty. I found someone carrying a lot of packages and I put on the brake, rolled down the window, and said, "Are you leaving?" I was surprised at how easy that was, but I was also mortified at the sheepish and desperately hopeful way it came across. A nice woman responded, "Yes, my car's over there." So I became just like one of these other parking lot weirdos and followed her in my car at a snail's pace. I could offer to carry her bags or give her a ride, but somehow that seemed inappropriate. Besides, she seemed perfectly content to have me follow her. She must have done this before, but I felt I had sunk to an all-time low. Once she put her bags in the trunk, she backed up her car, smiled and waved, and I pulled into the spot. I was overcome by a perverse feeling of accomplishment as I watched all of the other drivers still looking for a place to park. I kind of wanted to yell, "Ha, ha, suckers," but somehow that didn't really fit the spirit of the season.

Once in the mall (and I did get the right side), I looked at the directory and found Tiffany's. It's on the second level, so I traipsed to the escalator and glanced back to make sure I remembered the entrance. I could see the headlines now, "Missing Physics Teacher Found in Fetal Position Crying in Mall Parking Lot."

I anticipated this Tiffany's thing all day. How hard could it be to buy a very special woman a very special gift from a very special store? As I approached Tiffany's, I saw a guard standing at the entrance. That should have been my first clue. When I entered the store, I was greeted by a woman at a podium with a microphone. "Hello, and welcome to Tiffany's. Have you been here before?"

I wanted to say, "Yes, of course," like I do this sort of thing all of the time, but I thought that would just end up with my embarrassment so I was truthful. "No," I replied.

"Do you know what you want?"

"No, I just thought I'd look first."

"Great, take your time, and when you find something that interests you, please come back to the podium and I will assist you in finding the next available sales representative."

That whole complicated procedure, well, that should have been my second clue.

As I began to look, I noticed all of the prices turned upside down. Do I need to say that should have been my third clue? This was turning into a nightmare. I was starting to sweat under all of the lights, and as soon as I took my coat off, the security guard kept his eyes on me wherever I went. *Smash and grab isn't my style, dude.*

I couldn't make a decision on what I wanted to buy, plus I realized I couldn't find something, run to the podium, have the Tiffany's greeter announce that a sales representative is needed, show me the price, try not to gasp, and then say, "No thanks," only to have the whole process start over again. I had to plan very carefully.

One of the bracelets was a chain with a heart on it. I think every other jeweler has knocked off this design, so there's no point in buying the "real" one. I know this detail because I've heard my female students talking about that bracelet. I kept looking and I came across some key chains. For a moment I thought I could give Deb one with my key attached to the end. No, too forward. One of the key chains had the price tag flipped over. One of the sales representatives must not have been careful when putting it back. I put my face close to the glass to get a good look at the little slip of paper. $145.00. I looked again to make sure I saw the decimal in the right place. Yep, the little key chain was one hundred and forty-five dollars. I decided at this moment that having this price tag turned over was not a mistake, but a genius strategy.

I will *not* be intimidated. I am a teacher and if I can make it through the last day of school before Christmas break after a fire alarm, standing in the rain, then I can make it through this trip to Tiffany's. I walked back to the bracelets and found one I liked, a silver band that clasped together in a figure eight. I walked to the podium and announced to the greeter that I was ready for a sales representative. She asked me my name and announced that Dan was ready for a sales representative. A young woman approached me and said, "Hi, Dan, I'm Kara. I'll be your sales representative." *I think we get the point.*

"Where would you like to begin?"

"I'd like to see a bracelet."

"Okay, then."

I pointed to the bracelet all the while thinking, *Don't gasp, don't gasp.*

"Oh, excellent choice! Is this for your fiancée or girlfriend?"

Hmmmm...I never thought of Deb as my girlfriend. I guess I just thought of her as *the one* and kind of skipped over everything else.

So that I didn't have to explain that I was buying this for a woman who I hardly knew, I simply responded, "It's for my girlfriend."

As Kara handed me the bracelet she said, "Well, she's very lucky. This is a beautiful bracelet."

I turned the bracelet around in my hand, and I was surprised by its weight.

"The bracelet is sterling silver."

"It's heavy. You're right, it's beautiful." I tried to make like I was admiring the bracelet, which to a degree I was, but I was also trying to find a way to discreetly look at the price tag. When I found it, I know a gasp came out of my mouth despite my previous efforts. So much for mind over matter. Deb was worth it; it was just surprising a little bracelet could cost so much. I should have known when I saw the guard at the door.

I think Kara was surprised when I said, "I'll take it."

Kara wrapped the bracelet in a little blue box and tied it with a white ribbon. I felt like a kid because I couldn't wait for Christmas so I could see the look on Deb's face when she opened this gift. I was walking on air when I left the store, and even after all that, I still remembered what exit to take. As I entered the parking lot, some poor chap in a car asked, "Are you leaving?" I felt a camaraderie with him. I knew what he'd been through looking for a parking space, and I knew what he would soon be going through looking for the perfect gift. I replied, "Yes. Yes, I am. My car is right over there."

<hr/>

The next morning, Christmas Eve, I had second thoughts about the gift. I don't know—maybe the Tiffany's bracelet was too over the top. Maybe I'd scare Deb off. I tried to put myself in her shoes. What if the roles were reversed? Imagine. Okay, so we just met. What would be an over-the-top gift for me? Phillies tickets. That's it; she gives me two tickets to see the Philadelphia Phillies play. How would I feel about that? I would love it—who am I kidding?

I still felt a little strange. I picked up the phone and called Mark. He picked up after two rings, "Speak." I've said this before, I like Mark, I just can't figure out how he gets the women.

"Hey, Mark."

"Hey, bro. What's up with you? I haven't heard from you in a while."

"I know. It gets a little hectic at school this time of year."

"Yeah, yeah, I've heard that one before."

"Are you feeling neglected?"

Mark can be so sarcastic. "Oh, no, not me. Why would I feel neglected by my best bud? I mean we haven't spent any time together in…"

I cut him off before he said "three months." "Look, I need some advice."

"Advice, from me? Are you sure this is Dan? My basketball playing, cross-country skiing, physics teacher friend Dan?"

"You're hilarious. All I wanted was some advice from a trusted person. I need some advice about a woman I met."

"You met a woman? Where? Why don't I know about this?"

"I met Deb a short time ago. She's an actress."

"Wow, an actress. Is she hot?"

"I would describe her as beautiful."

"Okay, that means she's hot."

"Anyway, we haven't spent much time together, but the time we have spent together has been, oh, I don't know how to describe it."

"Have you had sex yet?"

"No."

"Then it can't be that great."

"Listen, not all of us men are like you."

"I am proud of who I am, I'll have you know. Not everyone can be a stud. It takes talent."

"My stud factor has served me well over the years, it's just that now it's honing in on one woman. Maybe I shouldn't ask you."

"No. Yes, you should. I'll cut it out. So you met a woman."

"Yes. And I feel a connection with her. Like I said, we haven't been around each other that much, but I can't stop thinking about her. There's something about her that I just love."

"Sounds like she could be the one."

"That's what I'm thinking and that's where I need the advice. We are planning on seeing each other for Christmas. Maybe not tomorrow, but sometime around Christmas. I just got back from the King of Prussia Mall."

"You went to the King of Prussia Mall?"

"Yes."

"Alone?"

"Yes."

"You must be in love. I'm really afraid of how you might answer this, but what did you get at the King of Prussia Mall?"

"I bought Deb a bracelet from Tiffany's."

"Thank goodness. I thought you bought an engagement ring."

"Not a ring, a bracelet. So what do you think? Is a bracelet from Tiffany's too much for someone that I just met?"

"Dude, anything from Tiffany's for any woman is too much. Are you nuts? She'll expect that treatment all of the time if you do it now."

"Hmmmm, that's what Nancy said."

"Nancy, who's Nancy? Is she single?"

"I work with Nancy, and no, she isn't single. Look, Deb isn't materialistic."

"How do you know? You just met her."

"You know, I didn't think I'd get interrogated by you. I just had a simple question."

"And I gave you my simple answer; it's just not the one you wanted to hear. I'm not trying to be a jerk here; I'm just telling you how I see this. You're a nice guy, Dan, and I don't want to see you taken advantage of. I don't want some woman using you for money. My best advice to you is to keep the bracelet until Valentine's Day. That way you'll know more about this girl and what she's all about."

"That's a good point."

"Yeah, it is. You're going to give it to her anyway, aren't you?"

"Yep." How could I listen to a guy who was still single and probably would be for the rest of his life? It's advice like that which keeps Mark alone. I know enough to follow my heart.

"All right. It's your life. So when do I get to meet this Deb?"

Chapter 7

Other things may change us,
but we start and end with family.
—Anthony Brandt

Once I finished telling Joel the whole story, there was silence on the other end. "Joel?"

"I'm here. I just can't believe this is happening."

"I called you because I don't know where else to turn."

"You need to let the officials up there handle this for now."

"I'll do that but I need your help, too."

"Of course I'll help. Let me just get my thoughts together. Let me tell Rachel about all of this, and I'll call you back. Are you okay, though?"

"Yeah, I'm okay. Talk to ya."

This was the type of story that I read about Monday mornings in the newspaper. This wasn't something that happened in my life.

My eyes were closed when a doctor opened the curtains and introduced himself to me.

"Hi, Dan. I'm Dr. Harper. You've had a rough time today."

Thinking of Deb I responded, "I'm not the only one."

"We've been in contact with the people at the ski resort, and we will let you know of their progress in finding your wife. I have your x-rays here and things don't look good. Your leg is broken in several places. We'll need an MRI to see if there is ligament damage as well."

I knew my leg was broken. *Big surprise.* I wasn't prepared for ligament damage, though. I wanted to get up and walk out of here so I could help find Deb, but after trying to stand when I was on the mountain, I knew that wasn't going to happen.

"You're going to need surgery. I will gladly do it here, but you will need to stay for a week. Where are you from?"

"Pennsylvania."

"If you have someone to drive you back, you can have the surgery there instead."

"No, I don't want to do that. I want to be here when Deb's found."

There was something in his eyes that I didn't like.

"You don't think they're going to find my wife, do you?"

"I didn't say that."

"No, but your eyes did."

"You're reading me wrong, Dan. I am concerned about both you and your wife. We need to get you healed and finding your wife is part of that process."

I knew I needed to be less defensive toward the people who were trying to help me. I changed my tone and said, "I'll have the surgery here."

"That's a wise choice."

Before the doctor walked out, he turned around and said, "Dan, everything will work out for you."

It sure doesn't feel that way.

After Dr. Harper left my room, my cellphone rang. "Dan, are you okay? I can't make sense of this." *That makes two of us.* "What do you need for us to do?"

It was my sister, Rachel, and she was on the verge of freaking out. I heard the same hysteria in her voice when our parents died.

"Rachel, I'm fine. I'll be okay. Don't worry about me. We need to concentrate on Deb."

"We're coming up there. Joel is trying to get plane tickets. We'll just rent a car when we get there. What hospital are you in?"

"Crawford, New Hampshire."

"Okay. We'll find it. Listen, Joel wants to talk to you."

"Who's involved in the search right now?"

"The crew from the resort."

"Have they reported this to the police yet?"

"I don't know."

"Where were you skiing?"

"White Pine Woods near Mount Washington."

"I'll look up their number and see what's being done. Hold tight until I call you back."

Dr. Harper walked back into my room and was a good distraction while I waited for Joel's call.

"I want this to be as easy as possible for you. After the surgery, I can probably discharge you in three days: the day of the surgery, and two after that to make sure everything is healing the way it should. You would be able to make the trip back to Pennsylvania if you stay over in Massachusetts. A five-hour drive is all that you could handle, and all that you would want to handle."

"How long can I wait until I have the surgery? I want to make sure that Deb is found."

"I'd like to get you in for an MRI today, and once I see the results, I can do the surgery first thing tomorrow."

"I can do that. My sister and her husband are on their way here. They're trying to get a flight. Would you please tell the staff? I want to know when they get here."

<hr />

All of my things sat on a chair next to my bed. I couldn't see anything but the curtains closed around me. As I was about to press the nurse's call button, one appeared with two cups. "Hi, Mr. Gallagher. I have pain relief medication for you."

"I don't want any painkillers."

"The doctor wanted you to have these."

The nurse looked at me with a bit of surprise. I guess there weren't many people who turned down pain medication. My leg was killing me and I wanted some relief, but not if it would make me fall asleep.

"Will they make me tired?"

"They might."

"What are they?"

"The doctor prescribed a medication that will give you a slow, steady release of medicine over time. It will relieve your pain."

"Can I take the lowest dose possible?"

"That's what we have here for you."

"I'll take it."

<hr />

Fifteen minutes after taking the medicine, my pain started to subside. My physical pain at least. It was dark, and I still had not heard anything about Deb. I called the nurse's station. "Yes, Mr. Gallagher."

"I need the phone number of the White Pine Woods Nordic Ski Lodge."

"I'll get it for you, Mr. Gallagher."

The phone rang a couple of times before a woman answered. "Hi, this is Sarah."

"Sarah, it's Dan Gallagher. Have they found Deb?" I was hopeful, but I knew in my heart what the answer would be. The hospital had been in contact with the resort and if Deb had been found, they would have told me by now.

"The guys are still out. They radioed in a few minutes ago. There are still two more trails in a remote part of the resort that they need to check, and it's taking some time in the dark. We are trying everything possible."

"Have you called the police yet?"

Silence on the other end.

"I have my answer."

"We were sure that we would find your wife by now."

"Sarah, we have to call the police now."

"I'll radio the guys and tell them your concerns, but at this point this case is just a missing person due to the elements, not a kidnapping. Look, I know this is upsetting. I'll call the police, but I can't guarantee what they'll do."

I hung up the phone, and the nurse walked back in to

check on me, "Is everything okay, Mr. Gallagher? I'm sorry, but I heard you talking on the phone."

"No, it's not okay."

My cell went off and on the other end Sarah told me that she informed the police and they would send a car over to be there when the search team returned.

The nurse said, "Everything will work out, Dan. It will be okay. Your wife will be found. I'll be back in a few minutes to take you for your MRI."

Looking down at my broken leg, I said, "I'll be here." *I promise I won't run away.*

———•———

I don't know why I didn't think of this sooner. I grabbed my cellphone and dialed Deb's number. I waited as it rang, and on the other end I heard her voicemail message. My heart sank a little bit, but it was good just to hear her voice. After the tone I said, "Deb. It's me. I don't know where you are or what happened to you. We'll get you help. There are so many people looking for you. I love you."

———•———

I sat back with the cellphone in my hand and held it to my chest, willing Deb to call me. I was still in that position when the nurse finally took me for the MRI. I had to keep perfectly still during the process. In order to do that I only let my mind focus on one scenario: The nurses will rush in and tell me that Deb has been found, safe. It's the only thing that can happen. I'll call my sister and let her know that she doesn't need to fly up here. Everything will turn out for the best. Just like it did when Deb and I first got together.

94

Chapter 8

Never worry about the size of your Christmas tree.
In the eyes of children, they are all 30 feet tall.
−Larry Wilde

I kept myself busy during the weeks that Deb was on tour anticipating the day I was supposed to call her, and finally here it was the start of Christmas break. I dialed Deb's number thinking about the possibilities our meeting might bring. "Hi, this is Deb…" same old routine as before, only this time I knew it was the answering machine. I left a message, "Hi, Deb, it's Dan. Time sure has flown by. I hope I can see you sometime over Christmas break." I wasn't expecting to see Deb tonight, but I was expecting to talk to her this evening. I needed to make myself busy again.

The running around at the King of Prussia Mall made me hungry. I put together a quick dinner, and while eating in the living room I looked around, wishing I had bought a Christmas tree. Since my mother died, I haven't had a tree. There's no need really. My mom died of cancer two years ago, and my dad died two years before her of a heart attack. My dad's death was difficult for my mother. Their marriage was like something out of the movies. I used to admire the way they looked at each other with such deep love, and I hoped I would find that same type of relationship for my life. When my mom was diagnosed with cancer, she didn't tell my sister or me. She only had a few months to live, and the doctors told us after her death that she didn't want to burden us with her illness. Rachel felt betrayed by our mother. She felt our mother robbed us of precious time with her. I think my sister just felt guilty that she lived so far away and that my mother didn't get to spend much time with her grandkids. I felt incredibly guilty, too. Perhaps even more so. My mother was only a few minutes away from me, but I still didn't see her or visit her as much as I could have. I just went on with my life, teaching, working out, and *teaching*. So, that's why I don't have a tree. I won't see my sister and her family until after Christmas, and my aunts and uncles are spread throughout the country. No real reason to get a tree just for me. The last two Christmases I spent alone. My sister asked me to stay with her, but I felt like it was important for her to spend it with her family. Don't get me wrong, I would have loved to see my nephews opening presents on Christmas morning, but it felt weird, so I just made myself a nice dinner and went to the movies. Christmas has been cheap for me lately, well, except for this year. Ah, back to thinking about Deb. It was almost eight thirty; I picked up a book and read for half an hour. At nine o'clock I glanced at the DVDs I still had piled up since last week. I was in the middle of reading the back cover of one of the movies when the phone rang. I grabbed my cell, my heart racing. "Hello."

"Hello, stranger."

"Hi, Deb, how are you?"

"Great. How are you? It sounds like you're out of breath."

"I was just doing some things around the house." *Not exactly a lie.*

"Oh, I'm sorry. I'll let you go."

"No, no, that's okay. It's nothing that can't wait."

"Oh, good. So this was your last day before vacation?"

"Yes, we have ten days off this year."

"How did the last day go? Were the kids all crazy, excited about their break?"

"The day was interesting, actually. The students were very good, all but one."

"Really? What happened?"

"First thing this morning the fire alarm went off."

"Yuck, it was raining this morning."

"I know."

"Were you soaked?"

"It wasn't too bad, but it was very chilly because I gave my coat away."

"Well, that was chivalrous of you. So there was a fire?"

"A small one in the boys' bathroom."

"No way. Did they find out who set it?"

"A girl."

"A girl?"

"Yep."

"That's weird, kind of smart though to set it in the boys' bathroom."

"That's what we thought, but we don't know why she set it."

"How long were you outside?"

"Not long. The administration let us come back in, but we had to separate into two big groups while the investigation was going on. I ended up in the auditorium."

"Was it torture?"

"No, it was actually kind of fun."

"Really?"

"Really. So, what did you do today?"

"Nothing as exciting as that. A few of my acting company friends came into town with me. They are heading up to Maine for the holidays, so they flew to Philadelphia with me and we spent the evening going out. They left this morning, but I stayed and went to the art museum. I just got back and saw that you called. I wasn't sure if you would remember."

"Of course I remembered. I've been looking forward to talking to you again."

"Me, too. I wish that we could have talked while I was away, but I was so busy traveling from one place to another."

"Does that get tiring?"

"Very, but I don't feel tired when I'm on stage. Or even right after. The adrenaline makes sure of that. It's usually the next morning when I feel like I can't get out of bed, but I have to because we are off to another place. It catches up with me after a while and sometimes I feel like I could just sleep for a day. I look forward to this time of year because it gives me a break."

"You must love the summer."

"I do, but not because I'm not working with the theater. I join the Renaissance Faire for the summer."

"Oh, yeah? Where?"

"Well, this year I joined one here in Pennsylvania. Have you ever been there?"

"I was there once."

"With school?"

"No. With my friends. We had a lot of fun."

"Great."

I knew I was changing the topic, "So what are your plans for Christmas? Are you going to see your family?"

"No, my mother died a few years ago, and I only see my father once a year on Father's Day, but I know if I just let that go and didn't call him that would be fine with him. He could care less about seeing me. He has his own life since my mother died, and it doesn't include me."

"I'm sorry to hear about your mom," and then I added, "and your dad."

"Oh, it's okay. I should be the one apologizing. It's almost Christmas, and you don't need to hear my sob story."

"It's not a problem. This is a difficult time of year for a lot of people. Reminders of Christmas and family are everywhere you go. For some it's a constant reminder of being alone."

"So what are you doing for Christmas?"

"Well, now would be the time for my sorry story."

"Oh, no. Not you, too."

"Unfortunately, me too."

"Why is Christmas difficult for you?"

"Both of my parents passed away."

"When?"

"My father died four years ago, and my mother, two."

"You've been alone now for two Christmases?"

"Right, how about you?"

"Five."

"That's a long time."

Deb said, "It's not that bad anymore, I'm pretty used to it."

I surprised myself with the ease I had asking the question, "Deb, would you like to spend Christmas together?"

———•+•———

The minute Deb said yes, my heart jumped and I started making winter wonderland Christmas plans, which included Deb coming over for dinner, which meant that I would have to run out to buy dinner, which meant I would have to fight the Christmas Eve crowds. Not a bad deal knowing that it was all for Deb. I decided on filet mignon cooked on the grill, baked potatoes in the oven and a head of broccoli steamed. I needed dessert, too. Maybe a frozen pumpkin pie? No, I'll order a pie from Stoudt's, coconut custard. I was all set except as I looked around my place, I noticed how drab it was. There wasn't a speck of festivity anywhere. Perhaps I should get a tree tomorrow, but that's no fun alone. Change of plans. I picked up the phone and Deb answered on the second ring, "Hi, Deb. It's Dan."

"Hi, Dan, I didn't expect to hear from you so soon."

"I didn't think I'd be calling so soon either, but I have an idea."

"Really? I'd love to hear it."

"When we got off the phone earlier, I looked around my house and realized how bare it looks. I don't even have a tree. So my idea is that we go get a tree tomorrow. Together. On Christmas Eve. I have some of my parents' decorations, and we could use those."

"That sounds like a wonderful idea, Dan. Thank you

so much! I had been dreading this Christmas, but then you invited me over and that made me happy. The only part that was making me a little sad was spending Christmas Eve alone, and now here you are again, my knight in shining armor! I am looking forward to tomorrow."

"I am too. I'll see you soon." Smiling, I hung up the phone thrilled that I could make Deb happy. The only change I made was to go to the food store right then so that I wouldn't have to drag Deb there on Christmas Eve. Focusing on the Christmas tree will make for a fun day.

———

I hardly got any sleep during the night, and as I stood on my front porch Christmas Eve morning with a cup of coffee I took a deep breath and sensed that there was snow in the air. I love that crisp, clean smell right before the first flakes fall. Deb arrived at my house while I was still outside. She waved and smiled as she parked her car in the circular driveway. The setting was perfect for her arrival; the white fence surrounding the property, horses frolicking in the meadow, and the strong, stately stone farmhouse with the smell of a fire in the fireplace coming out of the chimney. Once on the front porch she said, "Oh, I hope I didn't keep my knight waiting for very long!"

"Not at all. Do you want a cup of coffee?"

"I'd love one."

Deb stood awe-struck in the living room, "Dan, this house is amazing."

"It's been in our family for over a hundred years. After my parents passed away, they left it to me."

My life was taking a good turn. It had something more than just work. No matter what happened, no matter where this was headed, I was going to enjoy every minute of our time together. I actually looked forward to Christmas morning, something I hadn't done in years. Ever since my father passed away holidays haven't been the same. My dad instilled in us the importance of tradition and Christmas embodied that. My dad would spend days setting up the train yard, and he always left one thing undone, the figures. That job was for my sister and me. A few days before Christmas my mom would make hot chocolate, and Rachel and I would sit in the kitchen and wait for the formal announcement from my father that he had finished the train yard. When we finally heard those magical words, we would run into the living room, pick our favorite figures, and place them around the town. Some ice-skated on a pond, some went sledding down a little hill, some stood on the steps of the church, while others sat on a park bench and listened to a brass band. Rachel and I got to stay up late that night, and we would marvel at the creation as we watched the train go round and round gently puffing smoke from its small stack. Then on Christmas Eve, my sister and I would put on a play for our parents. Even into adulthood, Rachel and I spent every Christmas with our mom and dad. Rachel would bring her boys and her husband and we would all sleep over at the farmhouse. My mom and dad thought it would be funny if Rachel and I would still put on a play as adults; we compromised by telling stories instead.

I was so lost in my thoughts that I didn't realize that we had finished our coffee quickly; it was so cozy just sitting by the fire and relaxing.

"I could sit here all day and talk with you, but I guess we better go for a tree."

"I can't wait to find a tree. Where should we go?"

"I'm going to show you how we get a Christmas tree in the country."

<hr />

We got into my Jeep and headed for Sheerlund Forest. We took all back roads to get there and once we turned onto Christmas Tree Road, it was a whole new world. Mansions were on our right and the Christmas tree farm was on our left, surrounded by a split-rail fence. We spied the horse-drawn wagon filled with people sitting on hay heading out to pick the perfect tree. We pulled into the packed parking area right next to a barn. There were a couple of out buildings here: one, a barn filled with ornaments and decorated trees, and the other housed Santa Claus and hot chocolate and cookies. As soon as we opened the car door, snow began to fall. Deb hugged me, "It's a winter wonderland," she said looking up and then leaning in to kiss me. We walked up the trail to the wagon and climbed onto the soft, warm hay with hot chocolate and cookies in hand. All the people in the wagon huddled together and the anticipation was high for the forthcoming journey down the path into the acres of trees. We were determined to find the perfect one. Our driver shook the reins adorned with Christmas bells and the jingling echoed out across the field. The wagon stopped and provided time for us to search for our tree. Each family was given a saw and everybody scattered out into the maze of trees. It didn't take us long to find the tree with our name on it, a ten-foot Fraser fir groomed and manicured from tip to the bottom of the trunk. It looked like it belonged on a Christmas card instead of out in the middle of a field. Deb held the tree and laughed at me while I crawled underneath and tried to make a straight cut. After a great deal of effort, it felt good to watch the tree gently fall to the ground carpeted with snow. I forgot to tell Deb that we needed to drag it back to the loading spot for the next available wagon. It took both of us pulling on the trunk of the tree to get it all the way down the path. As we laughed at our toiling with the snow falling all around us, I couldn't help but think that this was the kind of Christmas I missed since my parents passed away, but here with Deb, I had it back again.

As we drove up the lane to my house with the Christmas tree secured to my roof, I glanced over at Deb. She looked happy and beautiful; her long brown hair cascading out of her hat was the perfect background for the white snow that collected on everything in its way. We carried the tree to the front porch before we went inside to make some hot chocolate and get a fire blazing again. Some traditional Christmas songs and hymns set the tone as we sifted through my old decorations. Deb pulled them out one by one.

Holding a crystal ornament up to the light, she said, "Dan, this is beautiful!"

"There's more of them in the box. My father used to buy a Swarovski crystal ornament for my mother every year. I used to wait for her to open the package at the bottom of her stocking. That's where my dad always used to put them. When she would dig in the stocking, her eyes were always expecting the velvet box at the bottom, and there it would be and delight would spread all over her face."

"That's so romantic. Were your parents very much in love?'

"They were. I saw myself having the same type of relationship that they had. They were best friends plus they adored each other. Some couples get used to each other and take each other for granted, but that wasn't my parents, and I admired them for that."

"It sounds like a perfect marriage."

"It was."

Deb kept digging for the crystal ornaments while I untangled the lights. "White or multi?" I asked.

"We decorated our tree with big color lights, so let's go for the small white."

"Done deal."

I finished straightening the cords, and then we set up the stand and filled it with water.

Deb asked, "Do you put an aspirin in the water?"

"No, do you?"

"Yes, but the needles drop anyway. I've also tried lemon-lime soda."

"Really? Did it work?"

"No, but I probably should have watered it!"

Deb was so cute and so sweet that everything she said melted my heart; I really wanted her to stay over tonight, but I didn't want to be too forward. This is a five-bedroom house, so I have plenty of guest rooms. I thought it would be romantic to wake up Christmas morning together. I glanced out the window and realized that Mother Nature had given me an excuse. "Deb, the snow is starting to pile up on the ground. Maybe we should get you home."

"I was looking forward to spending the day with you. If I'm not being too forward, I still have my suitcase in my car from my trip. Why don't I get it so that we can have an old-fashioned sleepover. What do you say?"

What do you think a guy would say?

We walked out to Deb's car together. "Dan, your house is so beautiful. With the snow falling it looks like a setting in a painting." We spent a few minutes walking around the property before heading back to the house.

When I opened the front door, a welcome blast of warm air hit us in the face. Deb took up her post at the ornaments, looking through each box.

She sounded filled with the spirit of the season. "It feels like an old-fashioned Christmas."

"I'll put the lights on the tree and then we can decorate. Would you like a glass of wine, some hot chocolate, or a soda?"

"I would love a glass of red wine."

I poured each of us a glass of red wine and took them out to the living room where Deb found a seat next to the fireplace. After I had the fire going, we sat and talked for a bit. Deb was an amazing woman.

She went to college for a bit to study drama, but then she got a job at a Renaissance Faire playing a pirate. Deb loved it so much that she stayed with them and quit school.

"What did you like about the faire? I mean obviously it had a great enough effect on you that you left college."

"If I had to narrow it down to one thing, it would be the live performance. It was so exciting. We had a little two-story theater for the pirate show. There was a balcony, several doors upstairs, several doors downstairs, and ropes hanging from above. It felt like play time or recess. We would chase each other with swords, run through those doors, and swing below on the rope. There was always a story that went along with the chase scenes. It was great fun; it hardly felt like work because I was getting paid to play. Although I wasn't going to become a millionaire on that salary."

"What else did you do?"

"I was the one who greeted the audience. I don't know how you teach high school because those shows were some of the hardest. We would have high school students sitting in the front row making comments, but the only nice thing was we could say whatever we wanted to them as long as we stayed in character. I learned very quickly just how to shut up a rowdy audience member, whether he was sixteen or sixty."

Deb's smile revealed just how much she loved the Renaissance Faire. Her whole face glowed as she told the story.

"What made you leave?"

"Perhaps I should save that story for another time. I've talked too much."

"Not at all. I loved your story."

"Dan, it's almost unbelievable that we are sitting here like this. I never would have guessed after we met in the parking lot that we would find each other again."

"I think it was meant to be."

Deb laughed and said, "I think you made it happen."

"That too. Hopefully you'll be happy that I made it happen."

I walked over to the tree, smiling and holding Deb's gaze, and picked up the lights. "I'll start at the top with these, and work to the bottom." Deb helped me by standing on the other side of the tree so that I could hand her the lights. Our hands brushed against each other and she didn't pull away or try to avoid my touch. That was a good sign; heck, Deb just being here was a good sign.

One by one we added the crystal ornaments to the tree. My parents actually had more than I remembered. Along with the crystal icicles, it's enough for the whole tree.

"Dan, the tree is beautiful."

Agreed. The whole tree sparkled and the lights reflected onto the walls. The room looked aglow with little lightning bugs. The flickering of the fire just added to the magic. Up until now Deb had been the one to touch me first. I didn't want to scare her off, but now standing next to her, I put my arm around her shoulders. "You decorated a beautiful tree."

"I couldn't have done it without your parents' ornaments." With each reflection of light dancing around the room, I could feel my mom and dad's approval.

I admired the tree for another moment and then asked, "Are you hungry?"

"Yes, I am."

"I have some filet, potatoes, and broccoli for dinner."

"Sounds delicious, can I help?"

"Absolutely not. You sit by the fire and enjoy your wine."

Deb looked through my CD collection while I put on my coat and headed outside to start the grill. The air outside was clean and crisp, and although it was only five o'clock, it was dark. The outdoor lights to my back patio reflected off the snow bringing a brightness to the evening, and I watched Deb through the window, amazed at the turn this day had taken. I looked around outside and enjoyed nature's frozen gift before going back inside. I heard James Taylor's Christmas collection playing.

Once back inside, I said to Deb, "Great CD choice."

"You have an unbelievable music selection. I chose a little something special for dinner, too. I hope you don't mind."

"I look forward to it."

"Are you sure you don't need any help?"

"Deb, you've already been a help. Just relax."

Deb smiled and continued drinking her wine by the fire. I took the steaks out to the grill. I will admit, steaks were the comfortable path for me. I knew they would taste great, but look impressive. I don't think she would be as impressed with my burgers. Inside I had the broccoli steaming and the potatoes had been in the oven for over half an hour. After I flipped the filets, I went inside to set the table, complete with candlelight. Deb was still sitting by the fire, but now her eyes were closed and I could tell she was completely relaxed. I took this moment to imagine us like this forever. Every snowfall, every Christmas, the two of us here together.

Through closed eyes Deb observed, "I know you're standing there looking at me."

"Does that bother you?"

"Not in the least. Please continue." Which I did for another few seconds, but I knew if I stood there any longer, we would be eating burnt steaks and that wouldn't be very impressive, so I rushed to the kitchen, grabbed the tongs, and headed out to the grill. The outside thermometer read ten degrees, but I still felt warm by how much I was drawn to Deb. I looked back through the window to take this moment in one more time, and she was on her cellphone.

I opened the door, "Deb, dinner is ready." She cut the call off quickly and I said, "A call from a secret admirer?" Deb laughed and replied, "That was just a friend."

We sat down at the table and like Deb promised, she chose perfect dinner music, Josh Groban. I bought that CD some time ago, but I don't listen to it nearly as much as I should. Along with the romantic music, might I add that dinner was just the right blend of easy and gourmet. Deb loved my cooking, and I loved watching Deb love my cooking. I gazed at her throughout dinner, forcing myself to remember I should eat too. In a time when I thought love wasn't going to go my way, everything seemed to be on my side. Our conversation came so easily to both of us, it was like we had known each other forever.

"So Dan, what made you want to be a physics teacher?"

"I always knew I would be some kind of teacher, but it took until high school before I knew I would be a physics teacher."

"What changed for you?"

"I had a wonderful physics teacher when I was in eleventh grade. I didn't realize it at the time, though. It took me until I had the same teacher for human physiology and medical terms in my junior year. It wasn't until then that I fully appreciated his teaching style and how much I was learning from him. I remember taking such extensive notes in his class that I never thought I would learn them. I used to sleep on my notebook, hoping that the information would somehow be absorbed through my pillow overnight."

"I think it's wonderful that a teacher influenced you so much. Did you ever thank him?"

"No, he retired before I got out of college. I never knew how to find him, but I thought of him often and all the help he gave me, especially when I had my own class sitting in front of me. Now that you know that about me, it's your turn. What influenced you?"

"I had the same sort of experience that you had. My musical director helped me so much. She helped me realize the kind of actor I could be. That's why I went to college for drama."

"Did you ever tell her how much she helped you?"

"No, I didn't. Remember I dropped out of college to join the Renaissance Faire. I thought she would be too disappointed in me to care that I had found a job."

"You know, I don't think you're giving her enough credit."

"I know you're probably right. She was an understanding woman who only wanted the best for all of her students. She always said that we needed to make our own way."

"And you did that! She would be proud."

Deb gave me a smile as both of us realized we should have given some of the people in our lives their just due. I guess Christmas has that effect on people, reminiscing and re-evaluating our past. I would have loved to spend another few minutes contemplating this, but dessert was waiting. I cleared our plates and made coffee. "Once the coffee is finished brewing, I have some coconut custard pie for dessert."

"You remembered! Oh Dan, you're the best!" *That's what I like to hear.*

The rest of our evening was spent listening to my CD collection. We sipped wine, sat close to each other on the sofa, and enjoyed having Christmas to spend with someone else. I'll skip ahead to what you might be wanting to know: *How did the Tiffany's bracelet go over?*

We opened gifts that night, our first Christmas Eve together. In the past, presents were always for Christmas morning, but this year was about making new traditions. I opened mine first. I was surprised. I wasn't expecting anything for me; I was too focused on my gift to Deb. But there I was opening a box that looked like a watch box. I couldn't think of what could possibly be in it. It was also very light, so I knew the gift wasn't a watch.

"You should not have gotten me a gift."

"I wanted to. The wrapping paper is a hint."

The paper was red and the bow was white. *A candy cane?*

I took off the lid to reveal two Phillies tickets for opening day.

"Are you kidding? Deb, this is perfect! How did you know?" *Phillies tickets! The perfect gift. I am in love with this woman.*

"Living this close to Philadelphia I knew that there was a good chance you liked the Phillies."

"You are a smart woman. I love the Phillies. I see that there are *two* tickets here."

"Yes, there are. Gee, who are you going to take?"

"Hmmmm…have you ever been to a major league baseball game?"

"No, but I would love to."

"Then it's a date!" Opening day was a few months away. Deb must have felt the same connection that I did. "Thank you, Deb. This is an incredible gift. Actually, it is the best gift I've ever received."

"You're welcome."

"Now it's your turn." I handed Deb the rectangle box wrapped in blue paper and tied with a white bow. I thought I saw a moment of recognition on her face, but I wasn't sure.

I watched Deb's face every second that she unwrapped the gift. When she opened the box and saw the Tiffany's bracelet she smiled. "Dan, this is perfect. I've always wanted something from Tiffany's. I just can't believe it. Thank you so much. It's so beautiful." I helped Deb put on the bracelet and then said something clever like, "Every girl should have something from Tiffany's." I heard that somewhere before. It might even be their ad campaign; brilliant, if it is. It made Deb laugh again anyway, a sound I love to hear.

⊷•⊶

The music, the tree, the snow, the laughter. Deb. That Christmas Eve was one of the most magical nights of my life and was the beginning of what I hoped would be a beautiful life together.

Chapter 9

Courage is resistance to fear,
mastery of fear—not absence of fear.
—Mark Twain

Once the MRI was over I wanted to be told that Deb was sitting in the waiting room. No one said that to me, though.

The technician wheeled me back to my room and before she left I asked, "Do you know who my nurse was earlier?"

"Yes. Her name is Bonnie."

"Will she be back?"

"I'll tell her you're asking for her."

"Thanks."

Only a few hours ago Deb and I were together, laughing and enjoying life. I felt a deep foreboding in my stomach like I was slipping away to a place I had never been. *I felt Deb's absence.* It was thick in my room like a heavy mist coming off the ocean on a cloudy day when it's impossible to tell where the sand, sky, and water meet. The whole ride back to the room I felt that thickness. The corridors, the walls, everything I looked at screamed *she's still out there.* Each time I replayed the scene on the trail with the mountain man, my heart stopped. I could tell by the look on Deb's face that his presence made her very uncomfortable. *His eyes said that he was an enemy.* I prayed to God that he didn't have Deb.

"Dan." It was Dr. Harper and Bonnie. "We have an update on the search for you."

Dr. Harper put his hand on my shoulder. "Unfortunately, Deb hasn't been found yet, and the temperature has dropped significantly since the sun set. The search party is going to work through the night to find your wife."

"What time is it?"

"It's seven o'clock." *Seven?* How did it get so late so fast?

Bonnie took my hand. "We are all so sorry you have to go through this."

Sorry. So sorry.

"I need to get out of here. I need to go back to the resort."

A look of worry covered the doctor's face. "You can't do that, Dan. You would be no good there."

"I would at least be near Deb. I'll pay for an ambulance ride back to the resort."

I could see the tension on Bonnie's face. "We need to get you better. Your leg's broken."

"I'll sign a waiver. It doesn't matter what happens to me. I don't care."

"You are not leaving here, Dan. No one will give you permission to do that. You could lose your leg. You have had severe trauma to your body, so a heart attack or stroke isn't out of the question either. You will be no good to Deb if you let your health deteriorate, and you might not make an ambulance ride back here in time."

I knew they were making sense. I didn't consider how bad my health was. Part of me wanted to fight against what the doctor and the nurse told me. I wanted to be the one who knew better, but I also realized that they were thinking about my welfare and I wasn't. The thought of losing my leg and then finding Deb sobered my thinking.

"You're right. My sister and her husband should be here soon. They could go to the lodge and keep me updated."

"We'll do our best to stay informed as well. We all want your wife found."

Dr. Harper said to me, "It would be a good idea to give you a mild sedative."

"Let me wait for my sister. I'll feel better once she is here."

Half an hour later I heard some commotion in the hallway and the sound of Rachel's voice.

Racing into my room, Rachel hugged me. "Dan, this is all so horrible."

"Rachel, Joel. Thank you so much for coming."

Rachel took my hand and Joel put his on my shoulder. "Rachel and I were talking on our way here. I think it would be a good idea if I went to the lodge. That way I can keep you guys updated."

Rachel added, "We spoke with the doctors and nurses. Everyone is so concerned about both you and Deb. They told us you wanted to leave. You need to take care of yourself too, Dan."

"I know. I've thought about that and I want to be healthy or at least on my way to being healthy when Deb is found. Joel, I would feel so much better knowing that you were there at the lodge. It will be nice for Deb to have a familiar face greeting her."

"I'm on my way, and please, listen to the doctors, Dan."

"I will."

"I'll make sure he does, sweetie." Rachel gave Joel a kiss goodbye and turned back to me. "Oh, Dan. I don't know what else to say."

"There isn't anything to say. I'm just so thankful that you and Joel are here. You have no idea."

Finally, I had some comfort. I never knew how much my family meant to me until that moment. When I was alone on the mountain and thought I'd see Deb soon, I was okay. Not great, but okay. When Deb wasn't at the lodge, I can't even explain it; but now I had some relief from that feeling.

Dr. Harper and his nurse Bonnie returned, and I introduced Rachel to them. Rachel said, "We've already met."

Dr. Harper smiled, "Your sister's here now, so time to get you some rest and reduce the stress on your body."

"Okay. Just please, any word let me know."

"Absolutely."

Bonnie took out a needle and gave me a shot of something. At first I felt like I could fight its effects, but there really wasn't any use. Rachel was talking to me, and the last thing I heard her say before I fell into a deep sleep was, "Everything will be all right, Dan."

 *Chapter 10*

*Sometimes you have to get to know someone really well
to realize you're really strangers.*
—Mary Tyler Moore

*D*eb and I were together for nearly six months when
I decided it was time to introduce my family and
friends to her. It had to be a big deal for most of the people
I know because I think they believed that I would never get
married. They thought that I would be a bachelor forever.

So once school was over and the summer was in full
swing, I decided to have a picnic. I invited my sister and
her family to stay with me for the weekend, and I invited
Mark, Nancy, and her boyfriend to my house for a regular
old cookout. I made hamburgers and hot dogs, nothing fancy, and I picked up a few cheese, fruit, and vegetable trays
from the local supermarket. I also made sure I had plenty
of snacks in the house for my nephews. Derek and John are
seven and ten and quite a handful.

When they pulled up the driveway, Derek and John es-
caped from the car before their parents and ran to me for a
huge group hug, "Hi, Uncle Dan."

"Hey boys, how are you? Are you glad school's out?"

"Are we ever!"

"Oh, you don't have to worry; September will be here before you know it."

"Uncle Dan, you say that every summer."

"I know, I know. I think it's funny."

My sister walked over to me, put her arms around me and said, "You're funny, all right!"

"Hi, sis. You look great. I guess Joel's taking good care of you."

"The best." Rachel shot a smile to Joel, who returned one that was just as warm. He shook my hand, "Dan, how are you?"

"Super, Joel. I'm glad you are all here. Why don't we go relax out back? Anyone need to use the bathroom?" Four hands went up.

"Okay, you know where they are. I'll get us some refreshments."

Then my sister said, "Is Deb here?"

"No, not yet. I thought we could all have dinner together. I wasn't sure how tired you would be from the drive, so I gave you some time to just relax. She'll be here soon, though. Mark's joining us too."

Rachel rolled her eyes. She was well aware of his bachelor lifestyle and often blamed him for my not being married. She jokingly referred to him as *her best friend.*

"I also invited Nancy and her boyfriend."

"Is Nancy your fellow teacher?"

"Yep, that's her."

"So, she's the one who made all of this happen. I can't wait to meet both of them."

I helped the boys get their bags out of the car and then served lemonade and sandwiches. The back of the house is relaxing any time of year, but I love when the weather is nice and I can sit out on my patio. A stream runs through the bottom of the property, right before the wooded part of the land. The sound of the water is soothing, and it is something I know my sister misses about this house.

When my mom passed away, she left the house to Rachel and me. The mortgage had already been paid off, but we were torn with what to do with the estate. Rachel didn't want it because she didn't feel like she could come back here and live peacefully since the death of our parents; there would be constant reminders of them everywhere. Plus, she didn't want to move the boys out of their school. I didn't want the house either. I liked my apartment. If I wanted to watch football all Sunday afternoon without any other responsibilities looming over my head, I could. Owning the farm meant managing a ton of property, not to mention the challenges of owning an old country estate, along with the time-consuming task of managing the horse stables. Rachel was heartbroken that I didn't want the house. She pleaded with me to take it. Even though Rachel felt like she couldn't live here, she had no problem if I did. She said that she couldn't bear the thought of our childhood home going to someone else. Rachel wanted me to have the house so badly that she even said she didn't want me to pay her for her half of the house. All she asked for was one hundred thousand dollars, but the house and the property were worth at least ten times that. I felt like I was cheating her, but she said it was a fair exchange for peace of mind. So there I was with a mortgage payment far below any rent payment ever was, but I had this beautiful property. If I ever sell it, I will make sure that my sister gets half. I had that agreement drawn up by an attorney. My sister said that it wasn't necessary, that we were family, but I told her that this would give me my peace of mind.

At first I felt overwhelmed with work. The grass alone took me an afternoon to mow.

Then I had this huge house to clean. I regretted the decision for about six months, but then I started to enjoy the property. I put Adirondack chairs down by the stream, and in the early morning I have my cup of coffee or in the evening a bottle of beer. It's quiet, and I love the nature that I have around me.

The first time I invited my sister here, I asked her if she felt uncomfortable. She said no, it still felt like home.

———

I just about had the table set when everyone came downstairs to help carry out the lemonade and sandwiches.

We sat around the patio table and Rachel started, "How was the end of your school year?"

"It was great. I had a very nice bunch of students."

"How do you always get such great students?"

"Because no matter what, I think they're great."

The boys wolfed down their sandwiches and ran off to look at the horses.

As they disappeared inside one of the stables, Rachel questioned me about Deb. "Okay, so tell me about Deb. She chose you, so that's a plus in my book right there."

"Well, Deb is an actress."

"We know that already. What else? How did you meet?"

"We met in a parking lot. She locked her keys in her car and my road service card and I came to the rescue."

"That's an interesting place to meet. So, did you ask her out?"

"Not exactly. That's where Nancy's help comes into the picture. I kind of found out where she was doing some plays, and I attended one of her performances and she happened to see me in the audience. She came up to me at the end and gave me her number."

Now it was Joel's turn to chime in, "That's awesome. She gave you her number." Then he turned to Rachel and said, "I just about had to beg you to go out with me. I would have died if you had given me your number."

"That's why I didn't give you my number, honey. I wanted you around for a little bit."

Even through their joking around, I could tell Joel and Rachel were a little run down. "Deb will be here around six for dinner. I know you two had a long drive; do you need a nap or a shower?"

Rachel and Joel agreed they could use some rest, and they headed upstairs for a nap. My nephews returned and plopped down on the sofa and were watching a very irritating cartoon. "Uncle Dan, do you have XBox or anything?"

"No way, guys! There are no video games allowed in this house."

"What? Uncle Dan, that's crazy."

"What's crazy is wasting so much time playing those things. Watching TV is a waste, too. How about you two come with me for a walk to the stream? We'll try to find some salamanders."

"Cool, let's go."

Exploring nature with my nephews helped pass the time. I was feeling very nervous about tonight. I had never made this big of a deal about any other girlfriend. Usually, my parents would have a family picnic and I would bring along a girlfriend. Now it seemed so unsettling because I really wanted everyone to like her.

My nephews loved the salamanders, but it was time to wash up. Deb didn't need to see me covered in mud. My sister and her husband were awake and refreshed, so they took charge of making sure my nephews were presentable. While in the shower, I couldn't shake my nerves. I don't know why; Deb is a wonderful person and so is my sister. They should get along just fine. I suppose I felt some apprehension because Rachel had been my only family for two years now, and I was finally planning on making an addition to it. I wanted everything to be perfect. Little did I know, that wasn't going to happen.

———

The doorbell rang about one hour later causing me the nauseating feeling of being punched in the gut. Derek and John ran to the door and stood at the threshold grinning. Before I could even introduce them, they said in unison, "*Hiiiii,* Deb." They can be so embarrassing, especially this time because it wasn't Deb at the door; it was Nancy.

"Hi, boys. I'm Nancy." She stuck out her hand.

Derek said, "It's nice to meet you. Sorry, we thought you were Uncle Dan's girlfriend."

"No, I'm not Uncle Dan's girlfriend. We teach together."

The boys stared at Nancy who was being blocked

from entering the house by my curious nephews. "You're a *teacher*?"

"Boys, let Nancy in." I walked over to her. "Hey, Nancy. It's great to see you." She gave me a hug. I was taken off guard because she'd never done that before.

"Where's your boyfriend?"

"He got a last minute call to go into the hospital. I didn't want to cancel; plus, I wouldn't miss this for the world."

"You just love this stuff, don't you, Nancy?"

"Yes, I do."

"So where's Deb?"

"She'll be here soon," and with that the doorbell rang again. The boys ran to the door, expecting to see Deb. This time it was Mark.

"Hi, Uncle Mark," they said in unison. Derek and John consider Mark their uncle because there was a time when he was always around. We would take the boys fishing and go-cart racing. Fun stuff like that. Mark doesn't have any nephews, so he thought it was cool to be an honorary uncle.

The only thing that Mark likes better than my nephews is a pretty woman. Nancy is quite attractive and as soon as he saw her, it was like no one else in the room existed.

"Well, who do we have here?" he said as he walked across the living room toward Nancy.

I jumped in, "This is Nancy. We teach together."

While shaking Nancy's hand, Mark bowed. "Nancy, it is so nice to meet you. I can't believe that Dan has kept us apart for so long."

"Nancy has a boyfriend, Mark. He couldn't be here because he was needed at the hospital. He's a doctor. What do *you* do for a living?"

"I'm also a doctor."

Nancy lifted her eyebrows, "Oh, really?"

"Yes. A doctor of love."

I stepped in to help Nancy out. "Nancy, just so you know, that's Mark's way of saying he's between jobs."

Nancy had a big smile on her face throughout the whole exchange, and Mark did not take his eyes off her once.

It was time for me to step in again. "Mark, there are children around. Behave yourself."

"I always do." Then leading Nancy into the kitchen, Mark asked her what she would be drinking tonight. I didn't feel the need to forewarn Nancy about Mark because I thought her boyfriend would be here, but now that she was a singleton Mark stayed close by. He tried to win her heart for the rest of the night. Poor Nancy. Come to think of it, poor Mark. Nancy's tough. She won't fall for his tricks.

Finally Deb arrived, and when she rang the bell everyone gathered in the living room and stood around like a human amphitheater. I could only imagine that Deb would feel like she was walking into the lion's den with this group. I really wanted to send all of them to the patio, but I knew they were excited for me, and besides, I doubt they would have listened.

Derek and John raced to answer the door. They performed the same routine again, "Hi, Deb."

Deb was a good sport. "Well, I must have made it to the big-time to have a couple of handsome boys like you two know who I am." They laughed and ran away. Thank goodness.

"Hi, Deb. I'm Rachel, Dan's sister." *Why does she do that? She always has to take charge.*

At least my brother-in-law let me introduce him. "And this is Joel, Rachel's husband." We made the rounds, and then walked through the house to the back patio. Rachel must have found my appetizers in the fridge because they were laid out nicely on the table. She also took the liberty of setting the table for me while I was showering. That just left the burgers and hot dogs for me to grill while everyone talked and while my nephews threw a football in the backyard.

I don't know why, but the conversation became somewhat strained between my sister and Deb. As the evening progressed, Rachel stared at Deb, and Deb talked to her, but wouldn't make much eye contact. Thankfully, Joel kept stepping in to fill the awkward pauses with stories of the boys, of me, and of questions about Deb's career, which she loved to talk about.

Once dinner was ready, my nephews carried their plates to the Adirondack chairs by the stream. Now that I was seated with everyone else, I could feel the tension around the table, all of it between my sister and Deb. It's difficult to explain exactly how Rachel acted toward Deb, but it was different than how she usually treated people. Rachel seemed very wary of Deb and she studied her like she was trying to decipher hieroglyphics. Deb wasn't at all intimidated by Rachel. She always answered her, but she wouldn't hold Rachel's gaze for long. Her lack of eye contact didn't come across as a lack of confidence, rather defiance. Deb knew she was getting the third degree from my sister, and she didn't want to offend me, but she wouldn't back down from her either. It was all very uncomfortable for everyone. It was like Rachel and Deb were the only two in the room and the rest of us…well, it was like we were the audience watching a play with a cast of two.

After dinner Rachel excused herself to clear the table and wash the dishes. Mark lent her a hand. When I went into the kitchen, they both had their backs to me. Neither one of them knew I was standing behind them, and to be honest I was going to announce myself until I heard the topic of their conversation happened to be my girlfriend.

Rachel started, "So, Mark, what do you think of Deb?"

"You obviously have your mind made up already, so why don't you tell me first?"

"There's something not quite right." I almost gasped out loud. *Not quite right.*

"What do you mean?"

"Well, for starters she won't look me in the eye. Her answers were so vague and things just don't add up."

"Maybe because you were almost interrogating her. All you needed was a metal chair and a spotlight."

"I wasn't interrogating her."

"Oh, okay. What do you call it then?"

"I call it being inquisitive."

"A child is inquisitive. Your questioning took on a different tone. I'm surprised no one got up and left dinner. Nancy looked horrified."

"I think Nancy looked interested in Deb's responses, and by the way, I like Nancy."

"Nancy looked like she wanted to leave."

"Well, I don't trust Deb."

"You just met her."

"Exactly! Why after six months are we finally meeting this girl?"

"Because she was on the road with her theater company."

"Yeah? Where else was she?"

"Rachel, you are being ridiculous. Let's just end this conversation now so we don't get into a huge argument. Just be happy for Dan."

Rachel didn't respond. She stood at the sink and continued rinsing the dishes. Mark turned around so I said, "Hey, guys," and acted like I knew nothing of what was said. "Rach, I'll get these."

Rachel's voice softened and she sounded like the sister I was used to. "Absolutely not. You did enough work for this dinner, which was delicious."

"So, what do you think of Deb?"

"Why don't I reserve that judgment until I get to know her better?"

"Fair enough."

There was a little hesitancy in her voice making me believe she thought that would never happen. I didn't want Rachel to outright lie about her opinion of Deb, but it would have been nice if she had done a bit more to spare my feelings. Instead of celebrating a successful evening and being on top of the world, I felt disappointed. Why couldn't Rachel just be happy for me, like Mark said?

Later when I walked Deb to her car, I asked what she thought of the evening. Deb didn't say one word about how Rachel treated her. Deb said she was happy to finally meet everyone that I've been talking about for so long, and that she loved hearing all of the stories about me. Deb did handle herself well around my family, but she *is* an actress.

Chapter 11

Days of absence, sad and dreary,
Clothed in sorrow's dark array,
Days of absence, I am weary;
She I love is far away.
—William Shakespeare

In the morning Bonnie came into my room and gave me another shot. It seemed like I had just had one, but the entire night passed by so quickly and without word of Deb. For the little time that I had before my surgery, I regretted my decision to have it. I thought I would be able to fight the effects of the medication, but I couldn't, and that made me feel even more out of control of this situation. Rachel stood over me. "I can't hear what you're saying. Just rest."

I felt like I was under water with all sound muffled. I was aware of everyone and everything my sister, the nurses, and the doctors said. I just couldn't tell who was saying what.

"They haven't found his wife yet." *God, I need to know where she is.*

"No, I didn't tell him." *I know she hasn't been found.*

"Better to wait until after his surgery."

"Did you see the paper this morning?" *Woman Missing Near Mount Washington.*

"I saw it. I feel so bad for him."

"Joel's still there. He sounded discouraged. He said that we need to stay positive, though, for Dan." *What about for Deb?*

"I hope they find her before he wakes up from his surgery."

"What if they don't?" *God, please let Deb be okay. If not, God, let me not wake up.*

From half-opened eyes, I saw Rachel pick up the phone. "Mark, it's Rachel. I have some bad news for you."

Chapter 12

We must be willing to get rid of the life we've planned,
so as to have the life that is waiting for us.
—Joseph Conrad

The morning after my less-than-successful cookout Joel and I drank coffee on the back porch, which gave me the opportunity to ask him without Rachel around what he thought of Deb.

He hesitated, "She's nice."

"Are you being honest?"

Joel's "Yeah," was not convincing.

"I don't think Rachel likes her."

"I'm not sure about that. She didn't say anything to me last night."

I couldn't believe Rachel wouldn't say anything to her husband about this whole thing. Joel would never let on, though, so I added, "Well, thanks for making dinner a lot more pleasant. Your intervention between them was a huge help."

"You're welcome. Being married for fifteen years has given me a lot of practice handling Rachel."

"You'd think I would have it down by now. I've known her my whole life."

"Yeah, but you're the younger brother. You don't stand a chance."

Joel had a point. Rachel did railroad me into taking the farmhouse. True, it's an awesome place to live and financially I'm set for life, but it all came at the cost of letting my sister make decisions for my life. I wasn't going to let her make this one. If the summer went well between Deb and me, and I expected it would, I planned to ask Deb to marry me. Once the ring was on Deb's finger there was nothing Rachel could do, or so I thought.

Chapter 13

Sometimes our hearts get tangled
And our souls a little off-kilter
Friends and family can set us right
And help guide us back to the light.
  −Sera Christann

When I woke up after my surgery, Mark was sitting on a chair right next to my bed. "Dude, you look like garbage. I know you broke your leg and everything, but heck."

I remembered my prayer to God. *Let me not wake up.* So here I was holding onto the belief that Deb was alive. I closed my eyes and slept for another three hours. When I woke up, the smell of coffee filled my room. Mark stood next to me with a cup of coffee in one hand and a sugar cookie in the other.

"Oh, dude, you're awake. This place is amazing. They have coffee and homemade cookies in the waiting room. I'd offer you some, but it's only for the visitors. Can you talk yet?"

I was still very groggy and in a lot of pain, but I mustered, "Yeah, I can talk."

"Bonnie, he's up."

My throat was scratchy, and I must have been whispering because Mark strained to hear me. "I see you're on a first-name basis with the nurses."

"They love me."

"I'm sure they do."

Bonnie came into the room. "How are you feeling, Dan?"

"Okay."

"You look better."

"That's not what Mark told me."

"Oh, don't listen to him. He's full of caffeine and sugar."

Mark took his hand holding the cookie and grabbed his heart. Crumbs flew all over the floor, and Bonnie hid a laugh. "You really shouldn't be eating food in here."

Mark shoved the entire cookie in his mouth, washed it down with the rest of his coffee, and threw the cup in the trash. "Eating? Who's eating?"

This time Bonnie laughed aloud and while shaking her head she said, "May I assume you're single?"

Bonnie turned her attention back to me. "Dan, this little button right here is a morphine pump. Press it when you start to feel too much pain. Okay?"

"I feel a lot of pain. I'll just press it now."

"It's going to make you tired." I dozed off to sleep and when I woke up, it seemed like hours had passed, but it was really only five minutes. I managed to talk to Mark during that time, but it took a while to get a full conversation out. Mark was very patient. "Dan, they haven't found Deb yet."

"I know."

"Joel picked Rachel up a little while ago. They waited until you got out of surgery, but they went back to the lodge. I made it here late this afternoon, and that's when they left. Rachel wanted to make sure you were okay. She's very upset."

"I know."

"No, I mean she's really upset. I think she feels badly for the way she treated Deb in the past. She didn't exactly make your engagement a picnic."

"Yeah. It's okay. I know Rachel only meant well. Things will be okay, Mark."

———

Deb's been missing for over twenty-four hours. I knew that was a bad sign. I pushed that thought out of my mind along with all of those missing persons shows I used to watch. I didn't want to remember that detectives always say if someone isn't found within the first twenty-four hours, it's not a good sign. I felt for the button on the morphine pump. There's only a certain amount that would come out each hour, but I didn't care. I pressed it again and again. I needed something to take away my pain. All of it.

Chapter 14

Family quarrels are bitter things. They don't go
according to any rules. They're not like aches or wounds;
they're more like splits in the skin that won't heal
because there's not enough material.
—F. Scott Fitzgerald

After the disastrous picnic, I kept Deb away from Rachel for a while. That summer went extremely well for Deb and me. She had two months of vacation over the summer, which gave us a lot of time to spend together. We went to the beach, Cape May, New Jersey, and stayed in a great bed and breakfast called the Angel of the Sea. It's two Victorian homes joined by a huge front porch. Deb had never been to a bed and breakfast; I never had either, but I remember Nancy telling me that her boyfriend took her there for her birthday and they had a great time.

The first day we arrived at two o'clock in the afternoon. We were told that tea and sweets would be served at four, and at five thirty, wine and cheese. We put our bags in our room and grabbed a few beach towels that they provided. We walked a few steps to Ocean Avenue, crossed the street, and found ourselves the perfect spot on the sand. The beach was glorious, hot with a cool ocean breeze. We spread out our blanket, put our towels on top, and headed out for an hour-and-a-half walk. When we got back, we were just in time to be first in line for the tea and sweets at the bed and breakfast. The entire house smelled like peanut butter cookies and coffee. I was truly in heaven. In the dining room a lace tablecloth adorned with bowls of fruit salad, trays of peanut butter cookies, and pans filled with chocolate cake beckoned me. I didn't know where to start. I mean, how many guests did they have? Should I take my fair share now, or try to save some for the rest of the guests? I went the conservative route, but I did go back for seconds, and after being so full I could barely move, I was happy for the long walk to counteract some of the calories.

After sitting on the porch for an hour sipping coffee, we went back to our room and watched the Phillies game while waiting for the next round of food.

The only thing better than the Phillies winning the game was the wine and cheese spread that the Angel of the Sea put out. There were several different types of crackers and the best cheese assortment I have ever had. They also made a crab dip that I couldn't get enough of. I was so full that I didn't think we would have to go out to dinner. We did eventually make it out to the beach again to watch the sun set over the ocean. That's why I decided to ask Deb to marry me at the beach. I had such a great plan to ask her, too. Once the summer was over, I thought we would have a nice autumn trip back. I was going to pack a picnic dinner for us, complete with a bottle of champagne for the 'yes' answer that I was hoping for. What happened with all of my plans is kind of a difficult story to tell. It has to do with both

Deb and Rachel. I don't know why having a girlfriend had to come along with so many problems. I finally found the person for me and my sister set roadblock after roadblock in the way to making Deb my wife.

My first mistake was talking to Rachel prior to popping the question. I wanted to tell her because I thought Rachel would be happy for me, or that I could at least make her happy for me. Shortly before school started I visited Rachel and Joel. I felt a little uneasy, and they could both tell something was up. After dinner and after my nephews went outside to play with the other kids in the neighborhood, I said to Rachel, "I have some big news to tell both of you."

Joel responded first, "You have our attention and support whatever it is." As Joel said the last part, he looked at Rachel.

I cleared my throat, "I'm going to ask Deb to marry me."

In one breath Rachel said, "Congratulations. I'll have a prenuptial agreement drawn up…at my expense of course."

Did I hear my sister correctly? *A prenup? Is she crazy?*

"What did you say?"

"You heard me, Dan. The two of you were spending so much time together, I figured this was coming. I can't stop you from marrying her—a huge mistake, I might add. I say that now because when this turns into a disaster later, you can't say that I never warned you."

"Are you kidding me? What's your problem with Deb? Or is it that your life is fine and dandy as long as mine isn't? I have listened to you in the past, Rachel, but not this time."

"You don't have a choice. There is no way that I'm having you lose half of our parents' estate because you chose a gold digger but are too blinded by the act she puts on to see it."

"A gold digger? Where do you get that?"

"She always has to have stuff—expensive jewelry, designer clothing."

"You have no idea who Deb is. She never asks me for anything."

"She doesn't have to—you're always there one step ahead with another extravagant gift for her."

"I am not."

"Yes, you are. I see it in her. If you didn't shower her with everything you do, you would be history and she would be out finding some other guy who would spend all of his money."

"You know what—there you go—it is *my* money and I will spend it how I want to."

"And that's fine because it is your money, but the estate is *ours*. It belonged to *our* parents."

"Our parents didn't have an estate. They had a horse farm."

"A *million-dollar* horse farm. Come on, Dan. Think about this. Take some time to let this really sink in. It makes sense. It's the smart thing to do. I handed this property over to you because you always loved it. Mom and Dad worked long and hard for this. Don't let all of us down."

"Joel, I thought you might stick up for me just a little."

"You know I usually do, but Rachel is making sense on this one, Dan. I agree with her. The one mistake that we made in this situation is that we should have talked about this when the house was turned over to you. Now it seems like bad timing. No matter who you marry, this is the right thing to do."

I looked back and forth between the two of them staring at me, willing them to change their mind. I had always been supportive of them, so why did they find it so difficult to make my life just a little bit easy?

"When I came over today, I expected some sort of argument or at least some displeasure with my decision. Whether or not I have your support, I'm marrying Deb. I'm happy for once in my life, truly happy, and I'm not going to let you take that away from me."

I got up from the table and walked out the door. On my way to my car I felt sick. Rachel was my only family left. What was I supposed to do if my future wife and my sister couldn't get along? And more than that, how was I supposed to ask Deb to marry me and then ask her to sign a prenup?

Chapter 15

"Hope" is the thing with feathers
That perches in the soul;
And sings the tune without the words
And never stops at all.
—Emily Dickinson

The phone rang and Mark picked it up and handed it to me.

"Dan." It was Rachel. "I might have some good news. Someone might have seen Deb."

"What? Are you serious?"

"Yes. We were all gathered around the front desk at the ski resort. A guy comes walking in with the newspaper and says that he thinks he saw the woman in the picture in the bar down the street. He really thinks he saw Deb. The police are questioning him right now."

I struggled to sit up in my bed. Seeing a glimmer of hope in my eyes, Mark kept asking me what was going on. "I'll tell you in a minute."

I gave Rachel my full attention. "Rachel, can you put this guy on the phone? I want to talk to him."

"I can't get him right now."

"You have to find out what he's saying to the police.

When does he think he saw her? Deb and I didn't go to any bars, so if he saw her, then it had to be after my accident. If he saw her, then she's still alive."

"I'll call you back when I can get ahold of this guy."

I could hardly contain myself. Mark said, "What? You have to tell me."

"A guy thinks he saw Deb at a bar."

"When?"

"I don't know. Rachel said the police are talking to him now, and she'll call me later."

Another hour passed before Rachel called me back. That hour felt longer than my stay on the mountain after I broke my leg.

Rachel put Joel on the phone. "Dan, I'm not sure if this is good news or not."

"Just tell me. Did he see Deb?"

"That's what I don't know."

"How can you not know? Either he saw her or he didn't."

"The picture of Deb that we got out of your wallet was perfect for the newspaper because it's so clear. The problem is that the woman this guy saw walk into the bar down the street from the resort was wearing a hat and a big, heavy coat. Deb gave her coat to you to sit on. That's one problem."

"Is he sure she was wearing a coat?"

"Yes."

"How does he know?"

"He said that she never took it off and it looked too big for her. He remembered because he thought it was weird."

"Did he see Deb's face or the color of her hair?"

"He said that he thinks the woman in the bar looked like Deb's picture, but he was unable to tell me how long her hair was because of the hat and because some of it was tucked in her coat. He said the face structure was the same."

"What else did he tell you?"

"Not much else. Just that after the woman walked in—"

"Deb. You can call her Deb."

"No, I can't, Dan. I don't know if it was her. I'm not going to give you false hope. I'll follow this lead the best I can, but if we think she was in the bar and she really wasn't, then we might be missing other clues. Anyway, soon after this woman walked in, a man came in and sat one seat away from her."

"Were they together?"

"It doesn't seem like it. They didn't talk to or look at each other. They also didn't leave together. They each had a beer. He finished his first and left. The woman was there for about five more minutes, and then she left."

"Did this guy see what kind of car she got into?"

"No. He stayed and had another drink. He has no idea what happened once she left. He said once he finished his second drink, he left. There were two vehicles in the parking lot; one was his, and there was one snowmobile, which had not been there before."

"Did the snowmobile belong to someone in the bar?"

"We're heading over to the bar now. I want to see if the snowmobile is still there—and if it is, who it belongs to."

"Call me as soon as you know something."

"I will."

Excitement and hope rose in me. I knew that was Deb.

Whatever happened to her on that mountain, we will get through it. The important thing is that she's alive. God answered my prayer.

Chapter 16

*You know you're in love when you can't fall asleep because
reality is finally better than your dreams.*
—Dr. Seuss

It took me a long time to come up with a plan
to counter the prenuptial agreement that Rachel
drew up. She did it on her own and had her attorney send it
to me. She also sent a letter along with it:

Dear Dan,

*All of our lives I have only looked out for your best interest. I
love you very much and in no way want to hurt you. I want you
to be happy, and I truly do hope that Deb is the perfect woman for
you. If the roles were reversed and I had our parents' house entirely
in my name, and then I decided to get married, it might make you
feel a little uncomfortable, too. I would be hurt if you wanted my
new husband to sign an agreement, but I think in the long run I
would see its value. I asked Joel if he would have signed one and
he said yes because he loves me. He also said that it would not have
affected our relationship. I hope your engagement is all that you
want it to be.*

Love, Rachel

So, I had the prenuptial agreement. Now all I needed was a ring and a plan. I took care of the ring first, knowing it would give me more time to think of a plan. I thought a Tiffany's engagement ring would show Deb just how much I love her. Tiffany's held special meaning for us because of our first Christmas together. I knew the ring would be a lot more than the bracelet, but I also knew what I was doing this time. No intimidation as before. And I also knew where to park.

A Tiffany's diamond was expensive, especially because I wanted one that looked impressive. I had a lot of money in the bank, and I couldn't think of a better reason to dip into some of it. I did do some research before I went looking for rings. I looked online and in stores, but once I went to Tiffany's, I was hooked. The sales representative let me take the ring out of the store, with a guard of course. I had read online that a Tiffany's diamond sparkles more than others because of the lighting in the store. That's just not true. I took the ring out into the mall, and the ring was just as beautiful. I decided on a one-carat, Tiffany's-style ring. When I left the store, I wanted to get home as fast as possible, call Deb and have her meet me for dinner. I knew, though, that I still had some more details to work out, so I would just have to be patient. I kept the ring in its little blue box and put it in the back of my closet. The next day I went to see my insurance agent. It was going to take a lot of money to balance out the prenuptial because Deb had no chance of getting one dollar out of the horse farm. My sister saw to it that it was a solid document.

Phil was my parents' insurance agent, and I kept the homeowner's insurance through his company. I went to his office two days after I bought the ring.

"Hey, Dan. It's good to see you. What can I do for you?"

"I need to take out a life insurance policy on myself."

"Of course. We will need to schedule a physical; we'll have a nurse come to your house. What amount were you thinking you want the policy for?"

"Five hundred thousand dollars."

"You want the policy for half a million?"

"Yes."

"Don't get me wrong here, that's great, but it is going to be expensive. You're still very young, which will help. What do you want this for? I don't remember hearing you had gotten married."

"I'm not, not yet. Soon. I bought the engagement ring a couple of days ago. I'm waiting to ask my girlfriend until I get this policy."

"Once again, I don't want to seem like you shouldn't have this policy, I'm just surprised."

I'm not sure why I told Phil all of this. Perhaps it's because everyone else in my life was so opinionated about *my* life. I just wanted some objectivity and maybe just someone to actually listen to my side of things. Phil's getting a lot of my money, so he had no choice but to be a captive audience.

"I know this visit is a surprise. There are some things going on in my life and that's why I'm here. As you know, Rachel signed the house over to me, and now that I'm getting married, she wants Deb, my future wife, to sign a prenuptial agreement. It's not very romantic to ask someone for their hand in marriage and then ask that same hand to sign a prenup. This is my way of countering. Having this prenup seems like I don't trust Deb, which is not the truth at all. Rachel doesn't trust her, which has made for an interesting couple of months. Anyway, the life insurance policy is just my way of saying 'thanks for signing the agreement.'"

"Rachel was smart doing this. Your parents left the two of you a very valuable piece of land. By the way, how is the property? Your parents did such a beautiful job maintaining the history of the house."

"Thanks. I tried to do the same, although I must say that I did turn one of the bedrooms into my man cave."

"A man cave is very important, no matter if you have an old house or a brand-new house. Listen, I will get to work on the policy, and I'll look at our nurse's schedule and set up an appointment time. Once I have the medical report back, I'll give you a call with the numbers, and we can meet then."

"Thanks, Phil."

"You're welcome. It was good to see you, Dan."

I only had to wait for a week and a half to get the paperwork from Phil. The insurance would be costly, but I was willing to pay the premium. It was the least I could do for Deb under the circumstances. Once I had the agreement in my hand, I gave the Angel of the Sea a call and booked Angel Suite 24. It would be a perfect room for a fall weekend. It's located on the second floor in the second house. It has a door that opens to a wrap-around porch overlooking the ocean. It also sports a king-size bed, a fireplace, and a big flat-screen TV. This was going to be a weekend to remember.

I called Deb as soon as I booked the reservation. "Hi, gorgeous. I have a surprise for you."

"Really? What is it?"

"Well, if you're free this weekend, I booked a suite at the Angel of the Sea."

"You're kidding!"

"No, I'm not."

"That is wonderful, Dan. This trip with the company has really worn me out. Plus, I miss you. This is just what we needed. We get to spend the weekend together and get some rest and relaxation time in too. Thank you so much."

"When will you be home?"

"I'll leave Thursday night so that I have time to do some laundry on Friday; otherwise, I'll have nothing to wear. When are we leaving?"

"Saturday morning."

"Oh, that's perfect, Dan. Thank you. I love the Angel of the Sea. We had so much fun there this summer."

"I know and we're going to have fun again."

I only had a few more days until we left, and I still had my shopping to do. I needed a bottle of champagne and a picnic basket along with some food to fill it.

———◆———

Each day dragged on, but finally Saturday morning arrived. Deb drove to my house and got out of her car with a huge smile on her face.

"Dan, you look great. Very handsome."

"Thanks, but you're the one who looks great. Are you ready?"

"Absolutely."

I grabbed Deb's very large bag and put it behind the second row of seats.

"A picnic basket and a cooler?"

"Yes. I picked up some snacks at the store. This afternoon is supposed to be beautiful."

Surprisingly, there was little traffic on the Schuylkill Expressway, but it was early. The river was on our left as we passed Boathouse Row and the Philadelphia Museum of Art. Only another hour until we were on the beach.

When we pulled into the parking lot behind the bed and breakfast, the sunshine and the smell of salt air filled the car. We were about four hours early for check-in, but it was worth a try. We walked up the stairs to the large wraparound porch and opening the door to the main house held a treat for our noses. Freshly brewed coffee and pancakes. Already, I looked forward to breakfast tomorrow.

"Good morning."

"Good morning. We have a reservation for today. Gallagher. I know we're early."

"Let's see. You're in room 24, an Angel Suite. The room is ready. Here's the key. The room is in the second house on the second floor. Do you need help with your bags?"

"No. I can get them. Thank you so much."

"You're welcome. Let me know if you need anything during your stay."

"We will. Thanks."

Deb practically ran to the Jeep.

I called after her, "I'll get the bags. Do you want to go for breakfast, and then for a walk on the beach?"

"Yes to both. I'm hungry, especially after smelling the pancakes!"

We drove to Stone Harbor for breakfast taking the Garden State Parkway. After crossing the bridge into Stone Harbor, we parked the car along Main Street and walked a block to the right, to a coffee house for bagels and coffee. The coffee house is a good place to go for a quick breakfast. It's crowded, but not as crowded as Uncle Joe's usually was in the morning, plus they had a great Bananas Foster flavored coffee, and both of us ordered a large. The décor is typical coffee house, mismatched sofas and chairs. It's small, but there's plenty of seating. A lot of parents bring their kids here and it was loud with ramblings of plans for their impending day at the beach. The kids weren't the only ones who were excited; I wanted that special moment when I popped the question to be a thing of the movies.

Deb noticed my preoccupation. "What are you thinking about?"

"Nothing really. Just what a beautiful day it is."

"It's gorgeous. I can't wait to get to the beach."

"I can't either."

"Order number twenty-three."

"That's us, Deb. I'll get the bagels."

The rest of breakfast was filled with chatter about the day's upcoming activities and with memories about all of the fun we've had at the Angel of the Sea this past summer. After breakfast we walked through some of the shops. There is a great glass store on the corner down from the coffee shop. Deb and I were careful not to brush up against any of the displays. Unlike the coffee shop, this place had no children running around. I found a book about sea glass, and it came with a little netted bag filled with blue and green sea glass. This was a nice start to my collection.

The drive back to Cape May seemed shorter than our drive to Stone Harbor. It must have been our full stomachs. The day was so warm that we would be able to get away with shorts and a sweatshirt once on the beach.

When we got back to the Angel of the Sea, I packed our bag with towels, sweatpants, and books. Deb folded the beach blanket over her arm, and I took care of the chairs. The beach is only a few steps past an historic inn and then across Ocean Avenue, which is always packed with cars in the summer and it sometimes takes a while to cross the street even though pedestrians are supposed to have the right of way. Today, there were no cars parked along the road and no traffic. With no one in either direction, we didn't even need to break stride. It was such a contrast to the coffee shop scene in Stone Harbor earlier in the morning. We set up our blanket and weighed it down with our bag and the two chairs. Taking a bottle of water, we started out for a long walk.

We headed to the right with the ocean on our left. All of the old Victorian homes with their rich colors and ornate architecture were on our right. We walked for a few minutes in silence just listening to the ocean, and then I asked, "How have things been for you?"

"Great. Work's going well. I love the traveling and doing

the plays, and now there is someone very special waiting for me when I return. How have things been for you?"

"I couldn't ask for anything to make it better. This year has flown by, and I can't think of even one bad time that we've had."

"I know. We never fight. We give each other our space. It's the ideal relationship."

I had my answer.

After a day at the beach, sitting, reading, and talking, we went back to our room and napped for a little bit. I woke a little earlier than Deb, showered, and got ready for the picnic. I packed all of the food from the cooler into the picnic basket, and I tried to be quiet but the champagne bottle and the glasses kept clinking together, causing Deb to stir.

"What are you doing?" My ruse was up.

"I'm packing a picnic for us. There's still enough of the day left to enjoy. The sun doesn't set for another hour and a half."

"You look great."

"Thanks."

"I need to take a shower. I've never had a picnic on the beach, so I want to look my best."

"You look beautiful already."

"Thanks, but I need a little freshening up."

This gave me a bit more time to get everything in place. I placed the Tiffany's ring box on the bottom of the beach bag and then put the blanket on top of it. Was Deb going to like the ring? That was the least of my worries; what I was really concerned about was the prenup, but that's for another day. I didn't want to spoil the moment with that discussion. Deb only took half an hour to get ready. She wore a black cashmere sweater that I bought for her and a pair of jeans that showed off her thin figure. I wore a heavy cable-knit sweater and jeans. Both of us slipped on flip-flops for the walk to the beach. It felt good to kick off our shoes and sink our feet into the sand. We picked a spot that was away from the entrance to the beach and close to the water. I was careful to get the blanket out of the bag because I didn't want the Tiffany's box to fall out. That would kind of ruin my plans. I opened the basket and pulled out the champagne.

Deb said, "You're kidding?"

"Absolutely not. This trip back here is a big celebration for us."

"Champagne on the beach. You are full of surprises, Dan."

Just wait. "Yes, well, the meal is simple. Sandwiches."

Deb unloaded the ham, swiss cheese, tomato, lettuce, and a small jar of mayonnaise. I had strawberries—even though they're not in season, I added a little sugar so they should taste just fine. I doubted this would fill us up, but my plan was to take Deb to the Lobster House for dinner later in the evening. I already asked one of the girls at the desk to make reservations for me. I told her my plan for the engagement; I wanted the best table at the restaurant, one with a view of the fishing boats and the lights.

I would love to say that this was the perfect moment, the exact type of moment that I planned, one that could be in the movies. I thought of everything. I had a plan for rain. I had a plan for if Deb said, "No." But this one thing I did not have a plan for: seagulls.

They can be annoying in the summer, begging and dive-bombing for food, but I was so focused on the engagement that I didn't even consider them a problem in the fall. So as Deb began to unpack the picnic basket, a swarm of seagulls landed in front of our blanket. Deb waved them off, and that worked for about a minute. They kept coming back. Waving at them didn't work. Getting up from the blanket and acting like I was going to run after them didn't work. This was turning into a disaster, a thing of the movies, the horror movies. It was like something out of Alfred Hitchcock's *The Birds*. When one of the seagulls walked onto our blanket and stuck its head into the basket, Deb said, "Maybe we should go back to our room." She picked up the beach bag with such force that the little blue box flew out and landed on the wet sand about ten feet in front of us. Eleven feet in front of us was the ocean, and as the surf started to roll in threatening to swallow the little blue box, I ran for it.

I heard Deb behind me, "What's that?"

I plucked the Tiffany's box from the sand, but not before a wave washed up over my hand and completely soaked the blue paper and white bow. This was not what I had planned. I turned around to see Deb standing on the blanket, "Dan, what are you doing? What's that?"

I walked a few steps back to Deb. "I wanted this to be a bit smoother than how it turned out."

"What are you talking about?"

I got down on one knee, wet box in hand. "Dan, what are you doing?"

"Deb, from the moment I saw you in the parking lot, I knew that you were the one for me. The one that I have been waiting for. I love you, Deb; will you marry me?"

Deb smiled, then laughed. "*Daaan!* I can't believe this. Yes. Yes, I will marry you!"

Deb wrapped her arms around me and we fell on the sand. Lying next to me she said, "So this is why you have been acting so strangely."

"You think I've been acting strangely?"

"Yes. Now this explains everything. I couldn't figure out what was going on with you. I can't believe this."

Sitting up I held the box out to Deb. "You still need the ring."

"A Tiffany's box. That's why you ran so fast."

"It's a little wet; do you want me to open it?"

"No, I'll open it." I watched as Deb untied the ribbon and let it fall from her hands. Her eyes widened when she saw the one-carat ring. "Dan, this is beautiful. You did such a good job picking this out."

"I wanted this to be special for you and Tiffany's was my first gift to you last year at Christmas."

"The ring is beautiful." Deb kissed me again.

"I wanted this to be memorable."

"It is, Dan; it is. Let's just take all of this stuff back and sit on the porch next to our room. We will still have an ocean view, but without the birds."

"Now that sounds perfect to me."

It was almost dusk and the wine and cheese party had begun in the dining room. Deb and I sat on two white wicker chairs and put our champagne on the glass table between us. We could still hear the ocean, and the moonlight reflected off the waves.

"We have reservations at The Lobster House."

"I love that place. What time?"

"Eight o'clock."

"So have you thought of what kind of wedding you would like to have?"

"No. My main concern was having you say 'yes.' I didn't even begin to think about the wedding. What about you? Do you have any ideas?"

"Not at the moment, but I'm sure I'll come up with something."

"I'm sure you will."

———•••———

Later that night at dinner I just couldn't get my mind off the prenup. It weighed heavily on me and I just wanted to get it off my chest, but I didn't want to ruin the moment.

"Dan, you look preoccupied again. What's wrong?"

"Nothing. I was just nervous about this weekend, and now I can relax. I guess I'm finding it difficult to do that."

"Just look at our view. The water is still, and the light is reflecting off it and illuminating the boats. It's a beautiful night."

"It is."

"What are you going to get?"

"I think we should get lobster; this is The Lobster House, after all."

"Let's do it."

Deb smiled; she looked happy. I decided to tell her about the agreement the next morning after breakfast. I had the prenup in my suitcase. *Romantic, huh?*

—————

The clanking of the dishes woke me up the next day. Even though we were in the second house, the kitchen window from the first house was near our room, and the noise wafted right up. I didn't mind it because I don't like sleeping too late, especially at the beach. There was just too much to enjoy. Waking up here reminded me of waking up in the morning after sleeping over at my grandmother's house. The smell of baked goods and of coffee brewing made me want to get dressed and make my way to the breakfast table; my heavy heart, though, compelled me to pull the covers over my head and go back to sleep. *Rachel. Why did you have to make things difficult for me?*

—————

After breakfast I felt like my heart was going to pound out of my chest. This could ruin everything. I had images of Deb grabbing the car keys and driving herself back to Pennsylvania. I had images of yelling and screaming and tears.

Once we were back in our room I said, "Deb, there's something I need to talk to you about."

"Okay, what?"

"Sit down."

"This sound serious."

"It is."

"Before we came here, I told Rachel and Joel about my plans to marry you."

"Okay."

"Deb, this has nothing to do with you, but Rachel is worried about our parents' property."

"What do you mean 'worried'?"

"She said that we should have talked about this before when she signed the house over to me. It's bad timing now."

"Well, what is it?"

"Rachel had a prenuptial agreement drawn up." *There, I said it.*

"A what?" Deb's voice sounded irritated as she stared at me.

"A prenuptial agreement."

"Yeah, I heard you. And what would I be agreeing to?"

"That in case of a divorce, you get no part of the horse farm."

"Really?" Now Deb sounded flat-out angry. "That's insulting."

"That's why I said it was bad timing. If fate would have been different, then whoever I would have married would be having this same discussion."

"Oh, that makes me feel better. You know, I don't like this at all."

"Wait. I don't like it either. I did something that I hope will help you understand that this agreement doesn't have to get in the way of anything that we have together."

"What could possibly do that?" Deb said looking down at her ring.

"I took out a five-hundred-thousand-dollar life insurance policy on myself. If something happens to me, then you get all of the money."

"Half a million dollars?"

"Yes. It's already signed over to you. You're the beneficiary."

"That was thoughtful of you. I mean, this is a little hurtful of your sister to do this, but I know you love me."

"I do. And I'm sorry about all of this. I truly am."

Deb's voice softened. "I know. I appreciate that. You must feel caught in the middle. I don't want you to have to spend our life together feeling that way. I'll sign the agreement."

I took the papers out of my suitcase and went through some of the details with her.

"Where do I sign?"

"I think we need to go to the attorney and sign everything in front of him."

"No problem. We will do that when we get back. I have a few days before I leave on my next play tour. How does that sound?"

"Good. I hope this doesn't put a damper on the engagement or our weekend."

"Absolutely not. It's a beautiful day and this is the start of our beautiful life together. Don't give that silly little agreement any more thought."

<hr />

Deb was understanding. Like she said, the rest of the weekend was wonderful. It was as if there was never a discussion about a prenuptial agreement. Rachel didn't ruin things for me after all. Deb saw to that, and I'm grateful to her for not letting this get between us.

Chapter 17

*It is a puzzling thing. The truth knocks on the door
and you say, "Go away, I'm looking for the truth,"
and so it goes away. Puzzling."*
—Robert M. Pirsig

"Dan, it's Joel. I know this is taking some time, but I wanted to make sure that I had everything clear."

"What's going on? Are you at the bar?"

"Yes. When we arrived the snowmobile was still here. The police traced the license plate back to a rental at White Pines. A man put his name down as Bob Jones, which is made up because the credit card that he used bears the name Rommel Hagan."

"*Ra-mel Hay-gen.* That's how it's pronounced?"

"Yes."

"Why would he use a different name on the registration?"

"I don't know. It does sound weird. But here's where it gets even weirder."

"What?"

"White Pines has surveillance tapes of this guy. The police made a copy and we're bringing them up for you to take a look at."

"How's that weird?"

"Let's just see if anything in any of the pictures jogs your memory."

———•—•———

Joel must have called the hospital staff because one of the orderlies brought in a VCR and hooked it up to the TV. Joel and Rachel, along with four police officers, arrived a short time later.

"Hey, bud. How are you?" Joel greeted me first.

"Great, now. I want to see the tape."

The image on the tape was of a man wearing what seemed to be a flannel shirt although the tape was black and white. Terror gripped me as I noticed his long hair. *It's the freak from the mountain.*

"That's him. That's the guy who has Deb. We passed him on the mountain and he stared at her. I felt so uncomfortable when he skied past us. I know that's him. He's wearing the flannel shirt and sweat pants. That's what the guy was wearing. Who wears that to cross-country ski?"

One of the police officers asked, "Are you absolutely sure that's who you saw?"

"I'm positive. I will never forget his face or his eyes."

I continued to watch as he rented the top-of-the-line cross-country equipment. So that explained why he had on ridiculous clothing, but expensive skis. I also watched as he bought a heavy ski coat. He had the cashier cut off the tags, and then he carried the equipment and the coat out the door.

Joel said, "That's all we have of him on tape. But we do know that he rented a snowmobile as well."

I thought back to the hour on the mountain. I didn't want to say anything; I needed to get this straight. I remembered hearing a snowmobile. But that was when I was rescued. That was at the end of my stay on the mountain. I knew I heard something else; the plane. That was soon after my accident though, and I was in shock after hitting the tree. I recalled being thrilled at hearing the sound of an engine because I thought it was a snowmobile. But then no one came and when I looked up I saw the plane. Now I thought maybe it was a snowmobile after all.

Rachel finally said something. "What's wrong, Dan?"

"I don't know. I heard things on the mountain. I heard a snowmobile or what I thought was a snowmobile soon after I broke my leg. I thought I was being rescued, but I was wrong." I didn't mention the plane to them. "What if the snowmobile that I heard near me was Rommel? What do we do now?"

"We have this guy's address. He lives in Mohnton, Pennsylvania."

"That's only fifteen minutes away from where I live."

"I know."

Chapter 18

*What greater thing is there for two human souls than to feel
that they are joined...to strengthen each other...to be one with
each other in silent unspeakable memories.*
— *George Eliot*

The anxiety over the prenuptial agreement just melted away. When we got back home from the weekend, Deb and I went to Rachel's attorney's office and signed the agreement. Deb never mentioned it again, and I tucked it away in my bottom drawer, a place where I would forget about it.

Deb came up with an inspiring idea for our wedding. I never would have thought this up on my own, but Deb did and I loved her all the more for it. We were out to dinner at one of our favorite places, Judy's on Cherry. It's a great restaurant in an old building—part of it, which is a tavern, actually looks like a log cabin. The rest of the building is brick. The restaurant is on the second floor and has wide-plank wood floors and a cozy feel to it. It was a Wednesday evening, I remember, because Judy's always has a pizza-and-wine-for-two special that night. Deb and I each ordered a personal pizza and a carafe of Chardonnay.

Once the waitress had our order, Deb said, "I have the perfect idea for our wedding."

"I can't wait to hear it."

"Let's get married at your house."

"At my house?"

"Yes. You have the beautiful property with the stream running through it. We can rent a big white tent and have it set up in the back yard. There's a gradual slope, but it levels out at the bottom. We can put candles along the stream and get married in the evening. We'll hang lanterns and white lights all over the place."

"It's a great idea, but will you be happy with that? I thought one of the hotels in the area might be more your style. It would be a little more formal."

"It just seems so impersonal. Besides that, having the wedding at your parents' house is more meaningful. It will be kind of like they're watching us."

I sipped my wine to relieve the lump in my throat. "That's very thoughtful, Deb. No wonder I love you."

"Great. So it's settled. We'll pick a date and I will start to work on everything. I'm thinking hydrangea—you have all of those beautiful bushes all over the place. We'll have the florist make up some gorgeous bouquets that will really set off the flowers that you already have."

"Whatever you want."

"Let's get married on the Fourth of July."

"That was fast."

"Everyone will have a holiday from work, so it doesn't matter what day of the week it is."

"Like I said, whatever you want. Just tell me when and

where, and I'll be there. I'll help you as much or as little as you want."

"I want your help. It is *our* wedding and I want it to be special for you too."

"As long as you're there, it will be."

———

We had less than a year to plan for the wedding, and we decided to stay with the outdoor idea and have it at my house, soon to be our home. We spent much of those few months making phone calls and putting our plans together. Rachel kept out of it and never asked me anything about the wedding other than the date. She didn't even respond when I told her that it would be at the house and that it was Deb's idea. I thought that might change her attitude toward Deb, but I was wrong. I was a little hurt at first, but once Deb and I were immersed in wedding details, I felt more energized about the future than upset about the problem with my sister. By April we had most of the arrangements covered. The invitations were ordered, the tent along with chairs, tables, and linens were reserved, and the caterer was paid for. As for the menu, we planned on a barbecue—steaks, shrimp, and salmon. I could just imagine us by the stream, smelling the steaks cooking, drinking a beer, and celebrating my marriage to my wonderful partner with my friends and family.

There were a couple of details that Deb took care of on her own. She picked out her dress, the cake, and the invitations. Deb did all of the mailing herself. All I had to do was provide her with names and addresses. I was grateful that she didn't want much help with this because I was in the last few weeks of school and trying as hard as I could to get all of the curriculum covered. I was incredibly busy, but part of me did feel a bit guilty for not helping with this huge task. Deb took on the cake and dress alone because she wanted them to be a surprise for me. I knew whatever the dress, she would look beautiful. Deb decided on sparklers for the favor. I did help with that. We spent a lot of time wrapping the sparklers in a light blue paper. The color was pretty close to the Tiffany's blue, and we topped each off with a white ribbon, also in the Tiffany's fashion. Even though our wedding was on the Fourth of July, Deb didn't want the color scheme to be a traditional red, white, and blue. We put a little twist on it. We discussed the music; it would be a holiday after all, and we weren't sure if a band would be available. In the end we decided to go with a string quartet to play during the ceremony and during dinner.

One evening in May, Deb and I were sitting on the Adirondack chairs by the stream, and Deb brought something up that I had not thought about.

"Who do you want to be your best man?"

"With everything else we've been doing, I haven't even considered that. Have you thought about your maid of honor?"

"I have no idea at this point."

"Well, what about some of your friends from Curtain Call Productions?"

"I thought about them, but they probably won't even be able to attend the wedding."

"Why not?"

"So many of them have other jobs in the summer, and they end up all over the country. It would be tough to ask someone to give up on that. You know we don't make a lot of money acting, so we have to do what we can in the summer to make up for not getting paid by Curtain Call."

"I hope some of them can make it, Deb. You spend so much time with them."

I didn't mean it as a negative comment, but Deb took it that way. "I know I spend a lot of time with them, but it's my job. I'm sorry I have a career that takes me away from you. What else can I say?"

"I know it's your job and you love it. I was just making an observation, not trying to get us in an argument."

"I think I'm just feeling a little overwhelmed. I didn't mean to get defensive."

"Well, then let me help you. Planning a wedding isn't easy."

"No, but I'll be fine. It's your busiest time of year, so I can handle it."

"Okay, Deb, but if you change your mind, I can easily transition into wedding-planner mode."

"As much as I would love to see you in that role, how about you just stick to physics teacher extraordinaire?"

"Now that's a role I'm comfortable with. Back to choosing a wedding party. Maybe we don't have to have anyone in the wedding. Maybe it can just be the two of us."

"You know what? That would be nice. All we need are witnesses and we will have plenty of those."

Over the next few weeks, Deb and I finalized our plans. My parents were good friends with the mayor of our borough, and he agreed to marry us on the Fourth of July. Our correspondence kept flooding in, and everyone was saying yes to the wedding; well, from my side at least. The weird thing was that all of the responses were from my family and friends and co-workers. No one from Deb's side responded at all. I realized that she and her father rarely spoke, and I've never met him, but I just thought that he might show up to give his daughter away. It was just odd, but I didn't say anything because I didn't want to cause any stress for Deb before our wedding. Deb spent weeks with the acting company; it irritated me that they wouldn't show up for the wedding. What kind of friends were they? We decided to seat my friends and family on both sides so that it didn't look awkward. We didn't want any empty chairs.

With everything in place there was only one detail left. I called the mayor and asked him if we needed anyone to stand up for us at the ceremony. He told me that we did not; we only needed witnesses and all of the attendees would have that honor. So, it would just be Deb and me standing at the altar together.

<hr />

Once school ended I spent most of my days making some minor improvements to the house. I did some painting and added a bit more landscaping. I also had the tent company come by and give me an estimate on hanging lights. The plans they had for hanging lights in the tent and around the property were intricate. It was going to look like a fantasy scene from a movie; I was assured Deb would be dazzled by it.

A few days before the Fourth, I picked up my tux. Mark went with me.

I put the tux on to make sure the alterations were correct, and while nodding his head in affirmation Mark said, "That tux looks sharp on you."

"Thanks."

"Are you nervous at all? I mean, I can't believe that you're getting married. That just leaves me. Hey, speaking of it just leaving me, will Nancy be at the wedding?"

"Yes, she will, Mark, but she responded that two will be attending. Her doctor friend will be accompanying her this time, so just behave yourself."

"All right. For you and your special day, anything. So how has Rachel been about all of this?"

"She has pretty much stayed out of it. Rachel will be there, of course, but she really offered no help, and she didn't make any comments about the wedding and reception being held at the house."

"Well, I think it's a great idea. It's a great start for your marriage. It's cool that Deb has embraced your parents' house. I know what the house means to you. Hey, remember when we were younger and we would hang out by the stream all day long to see what we could find lurking beneath rocks or hiding in the plant life? And there was nothing better on a hot summer day than swimming in that deep part right at the bend. Remember?"

"Oh, man, I haven't gone swimming in the stream for a long time. It was the perfect spot. Do you remember playing flashlight tag at night? When it was time to go inside, we were always too tired to complain."

"Your parents were great. It would have been nice to have them here for this special day."

"I know, but my parents left behind memories for all of us in every corner of this home and I finally appreciate what they built inside these walls. Their legacy is still here. For all of us."

Mark agreed, "The horse farm is a special place. We had fun times there. We still do."

"Only now we sit in Adirondack chairs and drink beer instead of running around like crazy kids."

"That's okay. Beer and a chair are more my speed at this point. Speaking of beer and a chair, do you want to go grab one now along with some lunch? My treat for my friend whose bachelor days are soon over."

"You make it sound like it's the end of an era."

"It is."

July third was full of activity at my house. The big white tent was set up at the bottom of the property near the stream. The lights were being hung and the chairs and tables were being arranged. Off to the side of the tent and immediately in front of the stream, all of the chairs for the wedding guests were set up. The tablecloths, the chairs, the lights, and the tent were all white. The cloth napkins and the china place settings were all the soft Tiffany's blue that matched the wrapping paper for the sparklers. I could see how all of this would come together, and Deb was right about the hydrangea. They were in bloom all over the yard, some blue and some white, and they tied in with the flower arrangements on the table. I had not seen Deb in a few days. Her Curtain Call friends threw her a bachelorette party and she stayed with one of them for a couple of days. She called and said that they were having some good girl-time. It gave her a chance to do some girl things like a manicure and a pedicure. Deb said that the bachelorette was more about that than partying. It was her way of connecting with her friends who could not attend the wedding. I was glad that she was having a good time, but I was going to be very happy to see her. When Deb finally pulled up to the house, she jumped out and ran to me. "The house looks incredible. All the decorations, the lights, the yard—it's like a fairy-tale movie set."

"That's what we were going for. How was your trip home?"

"Good. It seemed like it took forever because I couldn't wait to get back here. I just can't get over this," Deb said as she studied the grounds.

"I have to hand it to you, Deb, you sure knew what you were doing with the color scheme. It's beautiful. I love seeing all of this come together."

"Did you get your tux?"

"Yes, I did, but you can't see it until tomorrow."

"Ha, ha. Well, you can't see my dress 'til tomorrow."

"It won't be too long now until we're husband and wife."

"It sounds weird to hear that."

"I like the way it sounds."

"I do too. It just seemed like this day was far away and now here it is. In less than a few hours, we'll be married."

"Why don't I throw some steaks on the grill and we can have dinner down by the stream?"

As the sun set and the workers began to leave, I set up a small table next to the stream. I placed one of the white tablecloths on the table and placed two white chairs next to the table. The yard was illuminated and transformed. While Deb changed inside, I spent a moment taking everything in. *This is what our new lives will be like.*

I put the steaks on the grill, and I suppose I was too preoccupied with my thoughts of our life together to notice Deb had already come out of the house and was sitting at the table. She had her back to me and was looking out over the stream.

"Hey gorgeous. You slipped down here without my noticing."

There was a strain in Deb's voice when she answered, "I've just been enjoying the sound of the stream."

"What's wrong? You sound upset."

As Deb turned around, I could see she had been crying. "Deb, what's wrong?"

"Oh, I don't know. I think I'm just being silly. I was in the house getting ready for our dinner and everything hit me and I felt overwhelmed."

"Everything has been taken care of. There's nothing left to do, so what do you feel overwhelmed about?"

"I guess I had such a great couple of days with my friends, and then I came back and saw the house and how beautiful everything looks—the lights, the tables, the flowers. When I went inside to change, the realization hit me that my friends won't get to see this or share this with us, and I felt sad. I thought I was okay with it, but it hurts that they won't be here."

"I'm so sorry about your friends not being able to attend the wedding."

"It was just one of those moments where all of my emotions hit me and I started to cry. I thought about my dress and how beautiful it is—I started to cry. I got ahold of myself, but then I looked out the window and saw you setting the table for us—I started to cry again."

"Why don't we have Mark take some pictures so that your friends can see everything as it happens?"

"That's a really good idea."

"Don't worry about anything. Tomorrow is going to be a beautiful day. We will make sure that your friends get to share it with us. Okay?"

That seemed to cheer Deb up. "Okay."

"The steaks are ready—would you like some wine?"

"Of course."

We spent the rest of the evening by the stream talking about our future. Deb left around midnight. She said that she didn't want bags under her eyes for our wedding. I could not sleep, however. I kept walking around the house. Tomorrow, all of this, the house, the horses, the land—I would share with my new wife. Everything my parents worked for, I was going to get to enjoy with another person. My life was taking on a whole new meaning.

I finally fell asleep on the sofa very early in the morning, only to awake to the sun shining through the window. It seemed like this day would never come, but here it was six o'clock and in a few hours the caterers would be here setting up. The wedding was at four, the hottest part of the afternoon. It was supposed to be a warm day but not unbearable. Deb planned to be here around noon. She said that she would call me before she arrived so that I didn't see her by accident. We decided to get ready in separate parts of the house. I knew I would not be able to get any more sleep, so I made a pot of coffee and took a thermos down by the stream. Even though I was anticipating the day, I couldn't stop thinking about how upset Deb was last night. I felt bad about her friends not being able to attend, and who knows about her family. She never talked about them—just a few things about her mom and dad. I thought it was weird that Deb's friends couldn't bother to come to the wedding, but they could throw her a bachelorette. I know Deb doesn't make a lot of money, and since her friends were single, they couldn't afford to miss much pay, but she was on the road with them all of the time. I even considered at times that might be a problem for us. The good news was Deb thought everything looked beautiful and she wished she could share it with her friends. I've never heard of friends not making a wedding because of work, but who am I to judge? I've been looking forward to this day and I feel confident that Deb and I will have a long, happy life together.

———

At noon my phone rang. "Hi, future husband."

"Hi, future wife."

"It's close now, sweetie. I am looking forward to all of our plans coming together."

"I am too. The caterers are here setting up the barbecue pit. It smells delicious and they don't even have any food on yet."

"I'm looking forward to eating. I know that a bride should not say that. I should remain all dainty, but I'm starving."

"Eat as much as you want—we can even make a plate for you before the ceremony."

"How about I wait and eat with the guests."

"You can do whatever you want—it's your day."

"This is *our* day."

"Yes, it is. Are you feeling better today?"

"I feel great. Your camera idea made me feel better. Besides, I'm marrying the most wonderful man in the world, so how can I be upset? The most important person in my life will be there—that's all that matters."

"That's sweet of you, Deb."

"I'm almost at your house."

"*Our* house."

"Okay, *our house.*"

"I'll stay out back until you have yourself settled upstairs. Do you want some coffee or anything else?"

"No, I'm good."

"I'll talk to you soon."

<hr />

The lack of sleep the night before caught up with me and I took a nap in one of the guest rooms to keep the master bedroom open for Deb. My parents had their bedroom renovated into a beautiful master suite; that was the only way that they changed the house. Deb had a big room and a huge bathroom to use for getting ready. The bathroom sported a huge Jacuzzi tub and a shower and floor tiled in travertine. All of the fixtures were antique bronze and there was a crystal chandelier hanging over the tub. I remembered my father saying that he didn't think hanging a chandelier over the tub was such a good idea, but my mother said that a light was needed; why not a chandelier? I also remember my mom wanted the new bathroom after taking their dream vacation to Italy and my father remarking on the cost of the fixtures that my mom insisted they import from Italy. He also said, "Anything for your mother." The bathroom was very upscale, but the travertine still gave it a rustic look. Thinking about my parents got me a little down for a moment. *I just wish they were here to share this with us.* My mom would have liked Deb, and she would be touched that Deb wanted to have the wedding here. My parents loved this place, and they loved sharing it with other people. With that thought I fell asleep and awoke an hour later to the sound of a car. I looked out my window and there was a black truck parked in the road across the street from the house. It annoyed me a little bit to have this guy take a prime spot from one of our guests.

It was going on two o'clock, so I jumped in the shower. Even though Deb and I decided against a bridal party, we did agree that Mark and Nancy would help greet the guests and I wanted to be ready when they arrived. Mark and Nancy were very honored to be included. When Mark bought me lunch the day we picked up my tux, we talked about why Deb and I were not having a wedding party. It just would have been too awkward with Rachel. I definitely would have wanted Joel in the wedding, but I doubted Deb would have wanted Rachel to stand up for her, and in all honesty, Rachel would probably have said no. Nancy talked about the wedding every day; she felt that it was all because of her that I was getting married. She reminded me of that once in a while saying, "Just think, Roomie, it was all because you helped me chaperone that trip you tricked me into taking."

At three o'clock I put on shorts and a t-shirt. Not exactly wedding attire, but I didn't want to sweat in my shirt. When I heard two more car doors slam, I walked outside to investigate. It was Mark and Nancy. Both came separately and solo. As I walked across the yard, they crossed the street. Nancy and Mark hugged me, but his came with a hard slap on the back.

"Thank you for getting here early. Having the two of you part of the wedding means the world to Deb and me."

Nancy and Mark answered in unison, "You're welcome."

I asked Nancy, "Where's the doctor?"

"Doctoring, as usual. He got called in at the last minute."

Mark winked at me. "This day is getting better every minute."

Nancy laughed and shook her head. "So what do you need us to do?"

"As people walk in, greet them, and if you want to show them to their seats, you can or they can just sit anywhere."

Mark answered first. "That's easy enough," and Nancy added, "Is there anything else you need help with?"

"No, we have all of it covered."

As the three of us walked inside the house, Mark looked back over his shoulder and said, "Who's the genius who parked right in front of your house?"

"I don't know."

"Do you want me to tell him to move?"

"No."

"You know I'll do it."

"He's not really troubling anyone."

"Is it one of the caterers?"

"I don't know who it is, Mark. Let it go."

"All right. All right. Hey, do greeters get to drink while they greet?"

"You want to drink before I say my vows?"

"I don't want to be sober when my best friend ties the knot."

Nancy chimed in, "Dan, we will be fine and Mark is not going to drink before the ceremony."

Mark said, "How about during?"

———◆———

It was getting close to four o'clock. Even though the house is old, it has central air conditioning, so I stayed put to keep cool. I watched out the window as the guests arrived. The black truck was gone, and in its place was Joel and Rachel's vehicle. I called to Deb, "It's almost time."

"I'm ready. Are all of the guests here yet?"

"It looks like the last of them have filed in."

"I will listen for the music, and then I'll see you by the stream."

"I can't wait."

As I walked down the stairs, Nancy said, "Dan, you look great."

"Thanks, Nancy."

Mark turned to me, "Are you ready, bud?"

"I am. Are all of the guests here?"

"They are seated and ready." Mark put his full attention back on Nancy. "Why don't I escort you to your seat and then, Dan, I can come back for you. I'll drop you off at the altar—kind of like I'm your designated driver."

"Sounds good."

I watched as Mark took Nancy by the arm and led her out the back of the house and down through the yard to where the guests were seated. Mark came back for me. "Are you ready?"

"Let's do this."

Mark and I walked around the guests so as not to use the center aisle, which was for Deb. Once we were in the front, Mark gave me one more hug with one more slap to the back. He walked to his seat, and I watched for Deb to appear out of the back of the house. As she stepped onto the patio, I noticed her long, brown hair swept off her face and hanging straight. She wore a short veil attached to a white silk headband. As she got closer to me, I saw that her make-up was light with a pink glow. It's no wonder why Deb is an actress; she's stunning. Deb's dress was a white silk halter dress, which highlighted her soft tan skin. She carried white roses tied together with a blue ribbon that matched all of the other blue that we used to decorate for the wedding. This is the woman I would be spending the rest of my life with. I felt blessed; I was the luckiest man in the world. Deb smiled as she walked toward me, and I had worn a smile on my face since seeing her emerge from the house.

When Deb was next to me, I took her hand. The mayor asked everyone to be seated. Even though I heard vows before at friends' weddings, I never took them to heart until now. When the mayor said, "Do you take this man to be your lawfully wedded husband..." And Deb responded, "I do," my heart skipped a beat. I've never been so serious about anything in my life. This was going to be the best marriage ever. I would do anything to make Deb happy, to keep her happy. When I put Deb's ring on her finger, it sealed our vows and was a sign to everyone that we belonged to each other. I never looked at anyone but Deb through the entire ceremony, but I could feel the support of the people I loved and cared about. When the mayor said, "I now pronounce you husband and wife. You may now kiss the bride," I took Deb in my arms, kissed her, and spun her around in the air. Deb laughed and the guests applauded. We walked up the aisle and waited to receive everyone. Mark and Nancy took charge of letting each row exit. My sister and her family were first. She gave both of us a surprisingly warm embrace and said, "Congratulations." As the guests flowed through the line, they continued to the serving area.

We thought it would be nice to have a cocktail hour after the ceremony so people could mingle and get something to drink before dinner. Our day was truly blessed when a breeze started to blow, cooling the temperature and carrying the music throughout the reception. Deb and I spent half an hour getting well wishes from all of our guests. The cocktail hour was a good idea, after all. Once Deb and I received the last guests in line, Mark was there with two glasses of champagne. We gladly took them. Mark bowed out and left the two of us alone.

This was the first time since this morning that we actually had time to catch our breath.

"You look beautiful, Mrs. Gallagher."

"Why thank you, Mr. Gallagher."

"I like the way that sounds. *Mrs. Gallagher.*"

"I like it, too. It has a very nice ring to it."

I gave Deb a kiss. "This is the happiest day of my life, and the good news is this is just the beginning of many happy days for us."

"Then we have a special life ahead of us because I can never remember feeling this happy and alive. Mother Nature even cooperated with us."

"The breeze has cooled everything down." I glanced over to all of our guests having fun and laughing. "Our guests look like they're enjoying themselves."

Deb looked around. "Yes, they are. I guess it's time to eat. I'm famished."

"You never ate anything earlier?"

"No. I wanted to wait to eat at the reception."

"It looks like Mark is ushering people to their seats. We should go take our seats of honor. Mrs. Gallagher, if you would take my arm."

"My pleasure."

Deb looked up at me and smiled. It was one of those moments that I captured like a photograph in my mind. I often thought back to that moment. The way the sun was shining on her face making it glow slightly pinker than her blush. The way her eyes lit up and wrinkled a little in the corner. The way she tilted her head to the side, making her hair fall from her shoulder. My heart stopped in that moment and when I look back, I think all of time must have stopped too. It was the one moment in my life that was so vivid that when the memory crept into my mind, no matter how hard I tried to keep it hidden away in a part of me that I didn't even know existed, I felt profoundly sad, and sometimes it took days for me to fully hide it again. Only then did the pain stop, but only for a little while.

Chapter 19

Alone, all alone
Nobody, but nobody
Can make it out here alone.
—Maya Angelou

After seeing the video of the mountain man, I just couldn't stay in the hospital any longer. "It's time to check out of here."

Rachel's concern showed on her face. "Dan, you're just getting over surgery. You can't leave now."

"I have to get back home and see where this guy lives."

Joel jumped in, "That's a job for the police. You can't even drive yet."

"I know, but Mark will take me."

Just then Mark walked in. "Where am I taking you?"

"We have a video of the guy who has Deb. We also have his address. He lives in Mohnton."

Mark looked concerned. "That's only a few minutes from you."

"I know. That's why I want to leave."

"Of course I can drive you home."

Rachel didn't like the idea. "Mark, we have to wait to hear what the doctor says. We just can't pick Dan up and leave without the consent from the hospital."

I hit the call button for the nurse's station. "Yes, Mr. Gallagher?"

"I am going to need to see my doctor as soon as possible."

"I will be right there."

Bonnie took in the whole scene: the police, my sister, Mark. "What's going on?"

Rachel answered, "Dan wants to leave."

"I'm not sure that the doctor will release you yet, Dan."

"I'm leaving with or without the doctor's consent."

Bonnie turned toward the door. "I'll be right back."

As soon as we were alone, Rachel admonished me, "You're being ridiculous. You can't leave. We will go back and check everything out. Besides, what are you going to do? What are you going to be able to accomplish? What if they find Deb here and you're all the way back in Pennsylvania?"

Rachel had a point. All of my thoughts had been with this guy and finding *him*. I lost my focus.

Joel said, "Listen. You need to stay here for a few more days. Let yourself heal. It's still early on in the search. Deb might still be in this area. Can you just wait it out?"

"Fine, I can wait, but I want to know who this Rommel is."

"I'll see what I can find out. Just give me a little bit of time."

As Joel left, my doctor came in. "So what's this I hear about your leaving?"

I felt stupid. "Actually, I'm staying."

My doctor asked, "Did you find out anything new?"

"Well, the police found a video of a guy we passed on

the mountain. We think he might be the one who has Deb."

"We have a very tight-knit community up here. This has everyone concerned. Just know that there are a lot of people out there who know this area very well. They are looking as hard as they can. It's good that you're staying. Your wife needs you here."

"I know." I wanted to say more to him, but I couldn't exactly get the words out. That would come later when everyone left and Bonnie stopped in to check on me.

Rachel added, "Joel and I are going to go back to Reading. The police up here will contact the Mohnton Police Department and see what they can find out about Rommel Hagan."

"Call me as soon as you know something…and drive carefully."

Mark reassured Rachel, "I'll stay here with Dan."

"Thanks, Mark."

Joel and Rachel said their goodbyes before heading out on the long drive to Pennsylvania.

Mark encouraged me. "I think it's good that you're staying. Deb hasn't been found yet and it hasn't been so long that you should be driving home."

"In some way I feel like I need to see where this guy lives. I need some sort of perspective on him, besides what I saw on the trail and in the video. I want to know what he is all about."

"What do you think Joel and Rachel will find? Do you really think he's there at his house?"

"I don't know where he is, but if we know more about him, we'll get closer to finding Deb."

Just then one of the officers appeared at the door. My heart sank when I saw him. His face strained with concern, "Have you seen the weather report?"

"No."

"There's a nor'easter coming through tonight. They are forecasting two feet of snow in this area. We have everyone possible out looking for your wife."

Mark offered, "Not everyone. I'll go with you."

The officer thanked Mark and then turned to me. "Dan. I want to prepare you for the worst. If we don't find your wife now, the odds are stacked against us after the storm. I guess what I'm saying is that this is our only chance."

"I understand. Thanks for everything you and everyone else are doing."

As they walked out, Mark looked back at me over his shoulder.

I turned on the weather and across the screen in huge letters was *Severe Winter Storm Warning*. I looked in disbelief at the mass of dark green moving across the radar toward our area. When bad weather was forecasted, I always anticipated seeing that mass of green when I was teaching. Snow days were great. Life was great. Now everything was falling apart. The map changed to the snowfall amount and over New Hampshire was the number twelve with a plus sign after it.

I closed my eyes and prayed. *God, please, please let Deb be okay. Please, God. I don't know what to do. Please help Deb. Please let her be safe. Stay with her and protect her. If Deb is out there in this weather, just let her be all right. Please let the search party find her. I need Your help.* I waited a minute.

Nothing. No response. No guidance. No hope.

I drifted off to sleep and in my dreams I saw Deb smiling and standing at the top of a hill. The sun shone on her like it did on our wedding day. Without warning she fell and slid backward down the trail. The sun was still shining. There was a sharp curve, which would be easy to make on skis, but Deb couldn't make the turn sliding on ice on her back. Deb was slipping toward a drop. If she went over, it would kill her. She grasped at imaginary objects along the trail. A tree branch. A root from a nearby shrub. No luck. Nothing. None of it was really there. The clawing left Deb's nails broken and bloody. Little drops and streaks of blood stained the snow like some sort of sick pattern plowed into a farmer's frozen field. Deb moved away from me so quickly, yet it took forever for her to fall over the edge. My dream transported me to the rocks below where I saw Deb's back and her hair. Her arms and her legs moved, but she couldn't fly. She fell faster and faster toward the rocks. When Deb hit, her back bent, broken in two. Her legs dangled on the other side of the rock and her arms stretched over her head. One tiny snowflake landed on her lips. I looked up to the sky as more fell. All color drained from her face. What was once red and full of life was now grey. More snow. A light layer covered her cheeks and her gloves. I watched as my wife disappeared, swallowed by the snow. With layer upon layer she became an invisible part of the landscape. No one would know that was my wife, that was my life. I felt a hand on my arm and heard the whisper of my name, "Dan." I didn't want to wake up. I wanted to stay here. At least I knew where she was—there under the mounting snow.

The voice grew louder, "Dan."

I opened my eyes. Bonnie was next to me. "Wake up. You're having a bad dream."

"What time is it?"

"It's three o'clock."

"So there's still a bit of daylight left?" I tried not to think back to my dream. Tried not to think of the sun shining on her.

"Do you need anything? A small dose of something to help you relax?"

I sat up the best I could. Bonnie handed me a small pill and a cup of water. I gladly took it, relieved that I was not by myself. Bonnie handed me a tissue and it was then that I realized my face was wet. I must have been crying in my sleep. I hated that dream. Every second of it. It was the worst dream I've ever had, and it became the one dream that in time would haunt many of my nights. I wiped the tissue over my face, and once my face was dry, Bonnie said, "Do you want to watch some TV?"

"No, thanks. Every channel keeps interrupting with weather warnings. How is it outside? Is it snowing yet?"

"It is. It's not bad, though. Just a light dusting."

"That's good."

"Yes, it is. Where's Mark?"

"He's out helping the search party look for Deb."

"That's a good friend."

"You're right about that. We've been friends since we were kids. He has always been there for me. He was there for me during my wedding."

"Your wedding. Tell me about that."

Bonnie was trying to occupy my time and keep my mind off of the search. Thinking back to our wedding day brought me a sense of joy for a little while.

———

"It was the start of the happiest time of my life."

"Where did you get married?"

"Deb and I got married at my house, which used to be my parents' house. They owned a horse farm complete with a century-old farmhouse. It was the perfect setting. Deb looked beautiful that day. We got married on the Fourth of July. We had sparklers for favors, a big barbecue, a huge white tent, and lights everywhere."

"That sounds like a lot of fun."

"It was. After the ceremony everyone ate while a string quartet played music for us. It was like something you would see in the movies although with the busyness of life, we forgot to pick out a wedding song. When the leader of the string quartet came over to us to ask what song he should play for our first dance, we just looked at each other and started laughing. We couldn't stop. Finally, I said, 'We trust you. You can pick it out.' He went to the microphone and announced that the bride and groom would be sharing their first dance as husband and wife. Everyone got quiet. All eyes were on us, and all of our guests were smiling."

"So what song did they play?"

My voice cracked a little bit, "What a Wonderful World."

Bonnie's eyes teared. "That was a perfect choice."

After a moment Bonnie asked, "What about the cake? Did you smash cake in each other's face or feed each other nicely?"

Bonnie smiled and I shook my head. "Gosh, I haven't thought about that for a while. Deb handled the whole cake thing. She wanted it to be a surprise for me."

"Really? You don't usually hear guys talking about the wedding cake."

"No, they don't. I wouldn't be either, but it had a special meaning in our lives. It was funny."

"Funny?"

"Well, for our engagement I thought it would be nice to go to Cape May, New Jersey, and ask Deb to marry me on the beach."

"That's romantic."

"It was supposed to be, but it turned out to be more of a horror movie."

"Oh, no."

"Oh, yes." This was what I needed, a distraction from reality. My brain worked faster than my mouth, "You see, I went to Tiffany's for the engagement ring." Bonnie's eyes lit up when I mentioned Tiffany's. "I had the box on the bottom of our beach bag. As soon as we unpacked the picnic basket, seagulls swarmed the blanket." Bonnie and I both laughed; actually, half laughed and half cried. "Deb grabbed the bag and I watched in horror as the ring box flew out and onto the sand as a wave was rolling in. I tried to get to it in time, but the wave soaked the paper, and all the while Deb had no idea what was going on."

"This is the craziest engagement story I have ever heard."

"I can't even tell you how crazy it felt. I spent a fortune on that ring. I don't know what I would have done if the ocean had carried it away."

"Are you a good swimmer?"

"Not that good. Well, the reason I'm telling you all of this is because of the cake. It was a warm day and the caterer kept the cake in a refrigerated van. When it came time for the unveiling, two of the servers carried it across the lawn and put it on a table. The wedding cake was a layer cake that looked like Tiffany's boxes piled on top of one another. There was a huge white bow on top made of icing. Once the caterers put the cake down, I could see there was a little twist to these boxes. The bottom layer of icing looked like ocean waves swelling around the base of the biggest box. Riding one of those waves was a little bride and a little groom. They were holding hands. I don't think anyone could believe their eyes. The cake was clever, silly, and beautiful all at the same time. And after this very long story to answer your original question, we did not smash cake in each other's faces. The thought didn't even cross my mind. Later that evening we were sitting by the stream, and Deb told me that she had the couple riding the wave because no matter what kind of rough spots came at us, we would always come out on top."

"The two of you will come out on top of this, Dan. You and Deb have an entire community of people praying for you and hoping for the best for you. Keep the faith, no matter what. Listen, it's the end of my shift, but why don't I stay until Mark gets back?"

"No. I'm okay. It would actually make me feel better knowing that you were home safe with your family before the weather gets bad. Thanks for staying with me."

"It was my pleasure. I enjoyed your story."

Once Bonnie was gone, I waited by myself for an answer. I couldn't help but think back to my dream. What if it was true? What if it was one of those premonitions that people have? What if the search party doesn't find Deb and I never know what has become of her? How could I go on not knowing?

Hours went by and it was finally dark. Most of that time was spent telling Bonnie stories of the wedding. Now I sat alone waiting for Mark and the officers. I knew what the answer would be, though. Several inches of snow must have fallen. That combined with the lack of light must have halted the search.

I picked up my cellphone thinking of the message I left her. I needed to try one more time. I dialed Deb's number. In only a few seconds I heard our wedding song playing in the hallway, "What a Wonderful World." It was Deb's ringtone. I closed my eyes as tight as I could. With all of my might I prayed—*God, please let Deb be the one with the phone. Let it be her in the hallway.* The squeaking of wet boots sounded on the newly waxed floor. I opened my eyes, keeping them fixed on the door. The song got louder and louder. *Please, God.* Mark walked into my room followed by an officer, who was holding a plastic bag with Deb's phone in it. Mark looked me in the eyes and shook his head, "We didn't find her."

The police officer asked me to identify the phone. I nodded my head. "Where was it?"

"It was off to the side of a trail close to where you had your accident. I need to take it in, see if we get any fingerprints."

This can't be happening to us. This is all my fault. If I had

not gone down that hill, none of this ever would have hap-
pened. Deb would be fine. We would be enjoying a glass of wine
by the fireplace in the main lodge. We would be talking and
reading or just sitting quietly. Anything but this. How does an
entire existence change in a second?

Without looking at anyone I told Mark, "As soon as the roads are clear, I want to go home."

"I understand. I'll get everything ready." After hesitating for a minute, Mark offered, "We looked everywhere, Dan. People on skis, on snowmobiles, on foot, all looking for Deb. Every inch of this place was covered. I'm sorry, Dan. I wish I had different news."

The officer said, "I'm going to make a few phone calls. Check some other hospitals, see if anyone fitting your wife's description has been brought in. I'll let you know if we find anything."

"Thanks, I appreciate it." There was no emotion in my voice, just a void. I wished I had not had that dream. I could focus better, focus on Rachel and Joel and what they might find back home. It was the only hope that I had now and it was the one thing that I could cling to. There were only two options: one left Deb dead on Mount Washington and the other left her in the claws of a monster. I'm going to live for the second one, and when I find him, I'm going to kill him.

Chapter 20

I never wanted to go away, and the hard part now
is the leaving you all. I'm not afraid, but it seems as if
I should be homesick for you even in heaven.
— *Louisa May Alcott*

The rest of that night I couldn't sleep, even with a sedative. I watched TV and the weathermen all said that the roads would be safe for travel by the middle of the afternoon. Apparently trucks were out all night plowing, and the de-icer that they put on the highways before the storm was helping as well.

Joel and Rachel got home in the middle of the night. They hit the storm in Connecticut and travel was very slow for them. Rachel texted me during the trip to keep me informed of their progress and so that I would not worry. They got home too late to check out Rommel's house, but they promised to drive by was soon as the roads were clear.

First thing in the morning, Mark showed up with two very large cups of coffee. As he handed one to me, he said, "Did you get any rest at all?"

"No. I was too anxious to get going."

"Let's not wait around then. This trip home is the next phase of our plan. Once we get going, it will bring us closer to Deb."

"I have all of my paperwork for check out. I'm just waiting for the nurse to bring me some pain medication and the wheelchair."

Mark stepped out of the room to look down the hallway. He waved to someone and a minute later the nurse appeared with everything I needed to make my exit. I wrote down the names of everyone who helped me so I could send them all a thank you letter. They really did all that they could to make me feel better—physically and emotionally. The way they took care of me and took their time with me eased my pain.

The nurse wheeled me out of the room and down a short hallway. We exited from a different area than when I first arrived, so I didn't get to see the Women's Club greeting party that Mark loved. In no time we were out the door. The first thing that hit me was a wave of the most frigid air I had ever felt on my face. The next thing that struck me was the depth of the snow. The plowed snow was in piles so high that I felt like we were in a rat maze. White covered everything. The last thing that hit me was a memory of Deb, of that dream. I pushed it down, out of my consciousness. Hid it away.

Mark had my Jeep running and the inside was warm. The passenger seat was as far back as it would go so that I could keep my leg stretched out. As Mark talked to a nurse, I glanced around the Jeep. Deb's luggage was in the back with her winter coat next to it. A moment of realization hit me. I was going back home with my wife's luggage, but no wife. The back seat was full of Deb's things, but I felt emptier than the day she went missing. When I put my attention on the hospital again, there was a whole group of people standing there. Mark climbed into the car. "Everyone came out to see you off."

"That was nice," I said as I waved goodbye.

The tires made a crunching sound on the snow as we pulled away. Once we were on the main roads, they were a little bit clearer, but they were desolate and silent. The silence outside permeated the inside of the car and Mark and I didn't talk for about half an hour. Mark knew what I was thinking. All of this snow and Deb might be out there in it. I watched the landscape, half expecting to see her running out of the woods toward the road waving her hands above her head yelling, "Here I am. Don't leave without me." *Don't leave without me.* How could I leave? How could I stay?

Chapter 21

Friendship is unnecessary, like philosophy, like art...
It has no survival value; rather it is one of those things that
give value to survival.
— C.S. Lewis

About three hours into our return home, Rachel called me. "Dan." The urgency in her voice caused me a moment of panic.

"Rachel, what is it?"

"Something weird happened and we don't know what to make of it."

"Where are you?"

"We're back in your area. We've been back since late yesterday but the roads were really bad down here, so we went to that address in Mohnton first thing this morning."

"And..." Hesitation on the other end. "Rachel, what happened?"

"Well, Joel and I drove by a small white house...I don't even know if I can call it a house, it was more of a cottage or something like a cabin, but there were lights on and a black pick-up truck parked behind the house."

"Did you go up to the house?"

"Joel did. He made me wait in the car across the road. I watched Joel go up to the house and when he knocked, the light in the front window went off."

"Did anyone come to the door?"

"No one, but there was movement inside. Joel stood there for a while and knocked a couple of times. He walked around the house and looked in some windows, but he didn't see anyone. It was strange, and I want to be honest with you, I was kind of scared."

"Why?"

"I don't know. I just didn't have a good feeling about that place. It was creepy. Like I said, it almost looked like a shack. It sits all by itself in the middle of nowhere. The nearest house is about half a mile away and that house is a mansion that sits on top of a hill. This little shack is at the bottom of the hill near the road. There are woods on both sides of it and across the street."

I wanted to hear from Joel, hear his expertise. "Rachel, can I talk to Joel?"

"Yes, he's right here."

Joel answered, "Hey. I know what Rachel told you and she is accurate with that, but there's more."

"What?"

"After I walked around the house, I wrote down the license plate number. I called it in and it's registered to Rommel Hagan."

"But that's not so weird since the address is his."

"No, it's not, but Rachel and I waited outside for about an hour and a half. Nothing. Then all of the sudden the truck comes peeling around the back of the house and heads up the street in the opposite direction of where we were parked. I started the car and turned around, but we lost him."

"Did you see anyone else in the car?"

"With the tinted windows we didn't even see him in the car. Everything happened so fast. I wasn't expecting it."

"Where are you now?"

"We're driving around right now trying to figure out where he might have gone. We're going to go by his house again soon."

"Good. If you find him, can you arrest him?"

"For what?"

"For taking my wife."

"Well, we don't know that he took your wife. I'm sure the police look at him as a person of interest, but I don't think they'll be crashing down his door any time soon. I mean, what do we really have to go on? We know he was in New Hampshire. Deb was skiing and then went missing. What connection does he really have to her?"

"There was that guy at the bar."

"That guy at the bar might have seen Deb, but he's just a local who might have been hoping to get some notoriety, and he really couldn't identify her for sure."

"I know, but how do you explain that a woman who looked like Deb was seen in a bar where Rommel Hagan's rented snowmobile was found?"

"I don't think the Mohnton police are going to arrest him for not returning the snowmobile. And the police up in New Hampshire are focusing a hundred percent of their attention on the search."

"So they don't buy the abduction?"

"I don't think so; my opinion is that they think it's far-fetched at this point."

"Well, they didn't see this guy up close. If they had, they would understand my concern. If they were in my shoes, they would be worried, too."

"We'll stop by the police department; I'll see what I can do."

———

I shared all of the details of the phone call with Mark and then I added, "As soon as we get back, I want to drive to this guy's place."

"We can do that, but remember you have a broken leg."

"I remember that very well; I can barely move."

"Let's see what Rachel and Joel find and then make our decision."

"Regardless, I still want to see this place."

Mark and I had about four hours left to our trip and it would be close to sunset by the time we got back, but I kept thinking about that house and wondering why Rommel would leave in such haste. I wished that Joel and Rachel had been able to track him down.

As we continued driving, I imagined the shack with dirty wood floors that had been stripped of all varnish and were down to the bare wood, impossible to ever get clean. I imagined a cold place with drafts coming through all of the windows and tattered curtains blowing with each wind gust no matter how light. Could Deb have been there? Was she in Rommel's truck when he drove away from the shack? Is she still alive?

Mark interrupted my thoughts. "What's running through your mind?"

"I keep thinking about Deb and where she is. What if we don't find her? What if we never know what happened to her?"

"Don't think that way, Dan. You have to stay positive and focus on getting Deb back safe and sound."

"I know that's what I need to do. It's difficult to be on this side, though. I would give anything to be where Deb is, to trade places with her."

"We'll get her back. Wherever she is. There are a lot of people looking for her."

"Yeah,"—I said sarcastically—"us. The authorities in New Hampshire think Deb has been the victim of a snowstorm. I don't think they took this Rommel Hagan very seriously. I do, though. I know it's just a gut feeling, but I remember very clearly how it felt to pass him on that trail. He wasn't right. There was something bad about him."

"Stay with your gut feeling. We'll find this guy."

Time passed by quickly while we talked about Deb and made our plans for when we got back.

Rachel called when we had only two more hours left to our trip. "Hey. We went back to Rommel's house and it's still dark inside. It looks like no one has come or gone from the house. The truck's still gone. Joel and I have been here for another hour and there was no activity here. We're going to go home. Call me when you get back."

"I will. Thank you for all of your help. Tell Joel I said thanks, too."

"I will. Take care. How much longer do you guys have?"

"About two hours, but it depends on how many more stops we make. This trip has been rough."

"You'll be home soon. Be safe you guys."

To pass the last two hours of our trip I thought about my conversation with Rachel. The next time I glanced out the window, the local mini golf was off to the right, so I knew we were only about ten minutes away from home. I said to Mark, "Do you mind driving by Rommel's now?"

"No, bud. I think it's a good idea. Let's put your mind at rest." Mark hesitated for a second and then added, "I mean, the most at peace it can be right now."

"Don't worry; I know what you mean."

———◆———

As we got closer to Mohnton and to Rommel's house, I wasn't sure what we would find or how I would feel. Mark put Rommel's address in the GPS. We traveled several back roads; it was dusk, but I could still see the landscape outside the car window. There was a local preserved forest filled with evergreen trees that went on for miles. After we passed the forest, there was a narrow bridge and we made a right over it. To the left was a horse farm surrounded by a split-rail fence. I could feel that we were closing in. The road wound around two more curves and then Mark slowed down at an intersection. "This is it. We make a left here and then Rommel's house is on that road. What do you want me to do?"

Every good memory that I had of Deb ran through my mind in one instant. All of the fun we had over the past two years, all of the memories that we created with each other that no one and no circumstance could ever take away flashed frame by frame in my mind for me to see. Each picture clear. Each image of Deb smiling and laughing. "Let's go. We drove all this way. I would rather be sitting in front of Rommel's house than sitting at home alone."

After driving down a short, winding hill there was a large pond next to the road on the left and nothing but woods off to the right. Mark slowed down and said, "Rommel's place should be on the right."

My heart pounded and finally the little shack that Rachel told me about was there in a small clearing in the woods. It sat about twenty yards off the road with a steep hill behind it. Someone had been at the house long enough to clear an area to park a few cars so instead of parking across the street like Rachel and Joel, Mark pulled into the driveway in front of the house. I reached in the back for my crutches, and once they were in my hand I opened the door. Mark looked at me. "Are you kidding me? There's snow and ice everywhere and you have a broken leg. Let me look around. You stay here."

Mark stood in front of the house examining it. He walked around the side of the house and then disappeared around back. With my car door still open and my crutch in my hand, I leaned over and climbed out of the car. The terrible foreboding feeling I had when Rommel passed us on the ski trail multiplied here.

Mark made his way around the entire house and appeared by the front porch and watched as I steadied the crutches under my arms. "What are you doing? Stop already."

Mark walked up the two steps to the front porch and peered through the windows.

"Do you see anything?"

"It's dark in there."

"Is the door locked?"

Mark glanced back at me, "What if he's in there?"

"He's not in there. Try the door."

Mark placed his hand on the knob and nodded his head. "It's locked. I'm going to walk around back again while it's still somewhat light."

I hobbled the best I could away from the car trying not to fall. That's all I needed—to break my other leg. I was unsure of what we were looking for. Some sign that Deb was here or maybe just something that told us who Rommel really was and maybe where we could find him. Mark emerged from the other side of the house. "Except for the tire tracks in the snow, it doesn't look like anyone even lives here. There's nothing here. No outdoor furniture. No grill. No broom or snow shovels lying around."

"Could you see in the house when you went around back?"

"I could see in through a crack in the shades. There isn't much in the house. Some simple furniture. No real decorations or anything."

"I want to take a look."

Mark grabbed my arm and took a good hold of my coat. "Let's go."

With Mark steadying my upper body, I could make it across the driveway. We took it slowly making sure my crutches were planted firmly on the snow, and soon we were on the back porch and I was looking through the window of the house of the man who probably had my wife. Mark was right about the furniture. In the kitchen sat a small round table with two wooden chairs. I could see past the kitchen into the living room. From the angle I had, I could only see a rocking chair in the corner.

Mark said, "Let's walk around the rest of the house and back to the car."

As Mark walked to the end of the porch, a rush of fury came over me. I balanced myself on my good foot and let my left crutch fall to the wooden floor. I grabbed my right crutch like a baseball bat, and with all of my strength I swung at the kitchen window hoping to shatter the glass for an easy break-in. Instead, it bounced off of the glass and as the crutch ricocheted back toward me, I lost my balance and fell. Mark turned around and ran over to me. "Are you crazy?"

A sharp pain pulsed through my leg and my back. Mark demanded, "Are you okay?"

All I wanted to do was get in that house. Ignoring the pain, I said, "We have to break in."

"Have you lost your mind? We can't break in there. Let's go."

"I'm not getting up until we break into the house."

"Well, I'm not breaking into the house. You can stay here. I'm leaving."

Once again Mark disappeared around the side of the house. I waited a minute, but I didn't hear the car start.

A few seconds later, Mark stepped onto the back porch and without missing a single stride walked up to the door and kicked it in. The door hit the inside wall and swung back toward him. Mark leaned over me and in one movement grasped the front of my coat with both hands and picked me up. I held onto the house, and Mark handed me my crutches without saying a word. Mark went into the house first and I limped in behind him. Mark found the light switch and turned it on.

I said, "Look through everything as fast as you can. Try to find some sign of Deb."

We opened every drawer and every cabinet in the kitchen. Nothing. A few utensils. Four drinking glasses and four plates. As we saw through the window, there was a small table with only a couple of chairs. Next we walked into the living room. An old green plaid couch and a side table. Mark opened the drawer to find coasters. Coasters. In a place like this? We headed for the bedroom. A queen-size bed, a nightstand and a dresser with a small TV on top of it. I started with the dresser, pulling open drawers. Just some men's clothing in each one. Nothing that would say that Deb was here and only the remote control for the TV was in the nightstand. The bathroom, which was off the bedroom, was also rather empty. Generic soap and shampoo. Mark and I rushed through the shack like the police were on their way, but standing in the living room, I had to make sure we checked every inch. "Did we check under the bed?"

"I didn't and I'm sure in your state you didn't either. Let's go."

Mark got down on his knees and looked under the bed. "It's clear except for the dust." And then a second later, he said, "Wait. There's a hair tie."

Mark stood up holding a generic black ponytail holder. I said, "Could be Deb's."

"Didn't you say Rommel has long hair?"

"Yeah."

Dropping it on the floor, Mark said "Well, maybe it's his. Some dudes where hair ties."

"Was there anything else under there?"

"I'm sorry, but there wasn't and we have to go."

We made our way to the kitchen to close up, but the back door wouldn't stay shut, so Mark took one of the kitchen chairs and jammed it under the knob. He turned off the lights and we started for the living room. Mark unlocked the front door and we walked straight out onto the porch. Anyone driving by would see us. Mark made sure the door was locked and then pulled it shut.

Mark grabbed ahold of me again as we made our way to the car. Opening the passenger side door, Mark finally spoke up. "Our fingerprints are all over that house. If we made some kind of mistake and this isn't Rommel's place, and the owner of this house comes home to find a broken lock and a back door jammed closed with a kitchen chair and decides to call the cops, we lie. We both lie. I don't care what kind of evidence is in that house. You and I were never here. We went straight to your house, period."

"We were never here." I suppressed the urge to say that I'm not wrong that this is Rommel's house, but Mark went way beyond the call of a friend and I didn't want to inflame him anymore, so instead I looked back at the house as we drove away. We gained some ground here. Even though there was no evidence of Deb, we could move on from here and look elsewhere.

I didn't know how I was going to feel when I got back home. Mark must have known how I was feeling because he asked, "Do you want to stay at my place?"

"No. You've done more than enough already, and to tell you the truth, I want to be at home. It will help me think of what I should do next."

The sun set as we made the short drive to my house. It felt like years since I had been home, but in reality it was only a few days. Usually pulling up to my house would have me feeling content, but now I felt grief. Mark shut off the motor and we just sat staring at the house. Mark broke the silence, "I'll get the bags." I noticed he was careful not to say, "I'll get your bags," or "I'll get Deb's bags." I thought those words in my head, though. *Deb's bags.* How many times over the past two years did I watch Deb pack her suitcase for vacations that we've taken together and for her trips with her performing group. I missed Deb on those trips, and we had several arguments about her job taking her away countless times, but it did make her homecoming even better. I let myself out of the Jeep while Mark was in the back lifting our stuff out. I realized I didn't even know where my keys were. Mark opened one of the pockets in the front of my suitcase and took out my wallet and my keys.

I turned to him, "You know, bud, you took care of it all. Thanks, man. I appreciate everything."

I lamely made my way to the front door with Mark beside me holding the keys and the luggage.

He declared, "Let's do this," as he turned the key in the lock and pushed the door open.

I was surprised, but it felt good to be home. I thought I would feel Deb's absence even more here, but I felt closer to her now than the whole time I was in the hospital. I wanted to stay in New Hampshire until Deb was found, but being home felt right.

"Do you want to make the downstairs your home base?"

"That sounds like a good plan. I won't be able to make the steps."

"What do you need from upstairs?"

"Some clothes, my pillow, and some blankets."

Mark came back with his arms full. He pulled the sheets off my bed. Mark threw everything on the sofa. "Here are your blankets and clothes. I'll make the sofa up for you."

"Thanks." I observed as Mark fit the sheets over the sofa cushions. He placed the pillows at the end of the sofa that would allow me to see the TV. He put another sheet loosely on top of the other one and layered a few blankets on top of that.

"Mark, you're an expert at that."

"I should be. Do you know how many women I thought I might have a chance with, but instead I ended up on the couch?"

"Too many to count?"

Mark laughed at that and then got serious, "Do you want me to stay here?"

"Thanks, but I'll be okay. Really. I have a lot of thinking to do and I'm tired on top of everything else we've been through today."

Before leaving, Mark gave me a hug and a firm slap on the back. "Call me anytime. I don't care if it's three o'clock in the morning. If you need anything, call."

"I will. Thanks again, man, for all of your help. I couldn't have made it this far without you."

As I settled on the sofa, Mark closed the door behind him.

Chapter 22

There's a stranger in my house
Somebody here that I can't see.
—Ronnie Milsap

This was the first time during this whole ordeal that I was truly alone. I sat on the sofa looking around the house. Although it was still filled with our belongings, it seemed empty. This house always had such a comfortable quality to it even when I was a bachelor. Having Deb made the farmhouse complete. She made it a happy home.

As I continued to stare into the hallway hoping to see Deb walk into the living room, my cellphone rang. My heart dropped to the floor. *Deb.* If it was my wife, my prayers were answered, but if it was bad news…I pushed that thought from my mind.

I reached across the coffee table and picked it up. I didn't recognize the number. "Hello."

"Dan, it's Nancy. Mark called me a minute ago. This is horrible. What can I do?"

I was totally taken aback by the call. I hadn't even thought of school or of any other part of my life but Deb. "Nancy, I don't even know. I haven't called anyone at school yet to tell them about all of this."

"I'll take care of it for you. I'll explain to the substitute coordinator that you won't be in for a while."

"Thanks, that would be a huge help; you have no idea."

"Do you need me to come over?"

"No. Thanks, though." Remembering the fall I took at Rommel's house, I added, "Besides I'm in a lot of pain and the doctors gave me sleeping pills before I left New Hampshire. I think I might take one soon."

"If you need anything, Dan, call me. I feel terrible about this. I'll pray for you and Deb."

"Thanks, Nancy. I would appreciate that."

"Take care, Dan. I'll call you tomorrow."

<hr />

I had completely forgotten about the rest of my life. How could I forget to call school? Thank goodness Mark called Nancy—although I had no idea why he had her number.

I fumbled through my bag for the sleeping pills and then using my crutches, I stumbled into the kitchen for a drink of water. Half of me didn't want to take the pill because I wasn't sure what dreams sleep would bring. All I wanted tonight was darkness in my head. If there was such thing as nothingness, that's what I wanted.

I settled on the sofa, turned on the TV, and while I leaned back covering myself with the comforter, I looked at the television but didn't really see anything; I knew there was sound coming from it, but I didn't really hear anything. *If I don't find Deb, this is what my life would be like. Empty.*

Something Nancy said crept back into my mind. *I'll pray for Deb.* In my own frantic state of mind trying to figure out what to do on my own, I forgot about that part. I closed my eyes, folded my hands and prayed out loud, "God. I don't know where Deb is. I don't know what to do, where to go, what to say. Please help me find the answers. Please help me find Deb, God. Please let her be safe. Watch over her and protect her."

I let my mind go and as the sleeping pills kicked in and I drifted off to a disturbed sleep, I heard a car pull up outside, but then I thought maybe it was just the TV. I tried to shake the effects of the sleeping pills as best I could, but I swore I saw headlights shining in through the window, although maybe it was the flickering from the television. Then, I heard voices. Lifting my head off the pillow, I looked around. Were they coming from outside the house? I strained my eyes toward the window and was startled by a shadow passing by. I turned off the TV, got down on the floor, and crawled to the coat closet to get my father's shotgun. I laid it across my lap and waited in the entryway. I heard the creek of the back door as it opened; my heart pounded against my chest after realizing my cellphone was across the room by the sofa where I had left it after talking to Nancy. There was no way in my condition that I could get to it fast enough and without making any sounds. The only choice I had was to stay put until I found out who was in my house. It only took a few seconds for a shadow to appear, creeping into the living room. I pumped the shotgun as a warning, and the sound of soles slipping and stumbling over the hardwood floors filled the room. I took aim and fired at the figure as it ducked and ran through the back of the house. I stayed low to the floor, not wanting to make myself a target. A car door slammed, and I quickly unlocked the front door and opened it just in time to see tail lights pulling away. I closed and locked the front door and crawled back into the living room to get my cell. Mark told me if I needed anything at all no matter what time to call. *Well, buddy, you are going to get a call from me sooner than you probably thought.*

Mark answered on the second ring, "What happened? You shot someone?"

"I think maybe I did."

"Dude, get off the phone with me and call the cops right now. I'm coming over." And then before I hung up, Mark asked, "Hey, are you all right?"

"Yes. I'm fine."

The police arrived in a few minutes, but the emergency operator made sure I had my gun down before the cops would enter my house. I unlocked the door for them, and they searched the house from the basement to the upstairs. Nothing. Once the house was secured, we turned the lights on and found the damage the shotgun had done to my living room wall. Mark showed up and sat with me as the police continued looking around. One of the officers noticed small droplets of blood making a path from the area around the sofa through the kitchen and out the back door. The officer said, "It looks like some of the pellets grazed the perpetrator." They collected evidence and asked me if I had any idea who might have done this. Thinking back to earlier in the day when Mark and I broke into Rommel's house and all of the fingerprints we must have left behind, I kept my mouth shut, recalling our earlier conversation and the declaration, "We lie."

Mark didn't keep quiet though. He shook his head and said, "Officers, we've had a rough couple of days." Mark revealed the whole story about Deb going missing and about our suspicions concerning Rommel. Mark even told them we went to Rommel's place, leaving out the part where he kicked in the door.

The sun was up by the time the police left my house.

I said to Mark, "Thank you for telling them the story."

"I had to. This is an opportunity. Now our local police know about the situation; they have a lot more information that they can share with the cops in New Hampshire."

"I bet when you left here earlier you didn't think you would hear from me so soon."

"You got that right, brother."

Chapter 23

Still round the corner there may wait
A new road, or a secret gate.
—J.R.R. Tolkein

Mark and I were still talking about the events that unfolded overnight when Joel walked in holding a bag of bagels, with Rachel right behind him holding a carry-out carton of coffee.

Rachel said, "Hey, Mark. What are you doing here? Did you stay over last night?"

Sliding the gun under the sofa I said, "It was a rough night."

Joel responded, "What's up with the shotgun?" and then looking over at the wall, he added, "What in the world happened here?"

"It's a long story." Now, it was my turn to fill in the details while Mark listened and drank his coffee.

When Joel walked outside to look around, Rachel said, "What's going on here, Dan? You're scaring me."

"There are just a lot of things not adding up. We have this guy who just happened to be in New Hampshire the same time we were there and he ends up living a few minutes from us. Deb disappears and we weren't that far from the lodge. We see that strange guy on the trail and then Deb is supposedly spotted in a nearby bar well after my accident. There's a massive search and nothing but her cellphone is found. And then last night someone breaks into the house."

"We insist on staying here tonight. We should have been here already."

Joel returned from his investigation. "It looks like the police were able to collect some evidence."

Rachel said, "What do you think's going on here?"

Joel said, "I made some phone calls yesterday and I sent Rommel's license plate, a still photo that we took off the surveillance video, and his description to police stations in the surrounding counties, as well as to those from here all the way up to New Hampshire. We are naming him as a person of interest in Deb's case."

——•——

I felt like I was watching someone else's life in some story that had gone terribly wrong. How did we get to this point? One minute talking and laughing. One minute standing on top of a hill, the next lying on my back with a broken leg. One minute looking at my wife, watching her full of life run away for help and seeing her for the last time, skis tucked under her arm with her hair swinging back and forth in cadence with her steps. How did I get here? How did these circumstances take me so far beyond what I ever thought would happen in my life?

——•——

I spent the next few weeks making phone calls to my local police and to the department in New Hampshire. Nancy and Mark were visiting with me one day when my sister and brother-in-law stopped by. Rachel and Joel obviously had some agenda when they came over and it involved asking questions about Deb, opening all the old wounds that I thought were healed.

Joel started, "What are some things that you can tell us about Deb?"

"Like what? You know all there is to know about her."

Joel delicately chose his words, "To put it a different way, how well do you really know Deb?"

"What do you mean 'How well do I know her?' She's my wife, for crying out loud."

Rachel interrupted, "I know, but what do you know about her past? Where she came from?"

I could feel the anger rise in me. All of this time I thought everything was finally healed between Rachel and Deb, and here my sister was still holding onto some sort of ridiculous grudge against my wife. I don't like to raise my voice, but I felt a wave of red fury start at my feet and pulse through my body, exiting my mouth in a bellow. "You know, Rachel, you have no basis for anything you're saying. There is nothing that you have to back up whatever low opinion you have of Deb. And speaking of Deb, the last person I thought who would have attempted a character assassination of my wife while she's missing is my sister."

Joel stepped in, "Dan, it's just that we're concerned about you and your well-being. This whole situation is so strange and there were things from your marriage that bothered us."

"So you and Rachel are experts on marriage now and I guess yours is perfect?"

"I'm not saying that, Dan. We just had concerns that Deb was away so much. It didn't sit right with us, and you talked to us about it as well, so we know it bothered you too."

"It bothered me because I missed my wife and I made enough money that she didn't have to work. She could have explored her acting career in different ways if she hadn't had that job. And I didn't share that with you so that you could judge us or our marriage. You know what, everyone get out."

Nancy and Mark sat on the sofa looking uncomfortable and fidgeting with the cushions.

Nancy tried to smooth things over. "Dan, everyone's trying to help the best they can."

Later, I regretted what I said: "Oh, you too, Nancy? You're an expert all of a sudden? You know, I don't need your two cents right now either and I'm not going to say it again—everyone get out."

I wish that at this point I could tell you everything worked out, but that wasn't to be the case. I spent the next three months in my house. I paced from room to room, looked out of windows, sat on the front porch, and hobbled down to the stream, all the while expecting Deb to appear in front of me. Three months after my injury I was finally physically healed, but we only had two more weeks left until the end of school. What was the point in going back? A long-term substitute had spent most of the semester with kids who were supposed to be my students. Why disrupt all of that because I was bored, and worse yet, lonely?

Nancy called once a day to check in on me and to give me an update about my classes. I looked forward to her calls. A few times she brought dinner over for me and we ate outside by the stream. On Nancy's first take-out dinner visit, she put two pennies on the arm of her Adirondack chair. She kept them there for a few minutes, making sure I noticed them and then she picked them up and threw them one by one into the stream.

I said, "Are you making a wish, Nancy?" and she smiled slightly and replied, "No. I'm getting rid of my two cents." Mmmmm…a pang in my heart. I never should have treated Nancy that way.

I looked Nancy in the eyes. "I was such a jerk that day. I'm sorry. I shouldn't have said that to you. You've been such a good friend; you didn't deserve that."

"No, I didn't, but don't worry. I forgive you, Roomie."

Nancy was quick to forgive and I was grateful to her for that. Those dinners were some of the few times when I forgot about my problems and we would talk and laugh for hours. I learned fast during this ordeal who my real friends were. Nancy was obviously one of them—and to think of all of those times that I wanted to make it difficult for her sharing my room. Nancy was always there for me. Like it or not, the *Good Morning, Roomie* routine did brighten my day. And I can't forget that it was because of her that I got to see Deb for a second time, something I was sure never would have happened without Nancy's support. *Deb.* She wasn't out of my mind. Never had been. I filled each waking moment with thoughts and memories of her. I still prayed to God for her safety and well-being. The loss I felt was beyond description. I was empty and nothing filled me. Nothing good, as least. Only despair. The more despair filled my heart, the more I felt myself falling into a place I wasn't sure that I could escape. I needed to get out of here. I needed to go away for a while. Nancy agreed to help with the horses during my trip. I don't know why, but I felt like I could share my plan with her. Maybe it was because she had been understanding and easy to talk to. I also told Mark my plan and he wanted to come with me, but I said that Nancy might need his help around the stables.

Rachel and Joel didn't know about my trip; they tried to be supportive but after that argument at my house, I'm not sure they knew how. They tried to keep me from losing hope, but day after day and night after night alone with my thoughts, the seed of hopelessness set in. It took root and before I was completely lost, I needed to go back to New Hampshire. I needed to retrace all of our steps on that fateful day and then from that spot where I last saw my wife and last saw my life, I needed to find the route that Deb might have taken and look for any clue to where she might be.

Chapter 24

And miles to go before I sleep.
   −Robert Frost

The morning of my departure Joel called me. "Hey, I just wanted to let you know that the police are listing Rommel as a missing person. There has been absolutely no activity at his house or on his credit cards."

"What does that mean for this case?"

"It's at least still open. He's on the radar now."

"Well, that's good. He's never been off mine, though."

"I know. Hey, what are you up to?"

"I was just heading out for a long drive."

"Okay, Dan. I'll be in touch soon. Take care."

———◆———

I decided to leave on a Tuesday; I figured vacation season wouldn't be in full swing for another week, and I didn't want to fight the weekend crowds. It was early June in Pennsylvania, which meant a bit of crispness in the air, enough to need a light sweatshirt. In a few hours, though, it would get hot and the chill of the morning would be gone.

I already packed for the trip. The main essentials—hiking boots, rugged clothing, a jacket. I hadn't made reservations anywhere. I figured I would just find some little place to park myself at night.

I walked around the house making sure everything was unplugged or turned off. I also made sure all of the doors were locked. Then, I threw my bag in the back seat and set out for a long car ride.

The landscape was so different now that I could see green grass, leaf-covered trees, and wildflowers growing alongside the highway. The last time I drove this route, Mark and I could barely see a thing over the snow mounds.

I arrived in New Hampshire in the late afternoon. I took my drive more carefully now. I needed to find a place to stay. One of the guidance counselors at school was originally from North Conway, New Hampshire. She had beautiful photographs of North Conway and Crawford Notch hanging in her office. The distance between the two is short, so I set out on Route 16 to find a place to stay. I realized that the few times I stopped during this trip were to use the restroom and stretch my legs. I had not eaten a thing since I left my house. There were a few restaurant options on Main Street, but I stopped at an inn. It looked like a lodge on the inside, complete with huge log beams supporting the ceiling. White tablecloths covered the small round tables, making a stark contrast with the light wood walls. An older woman, very well dressed, showed me to my seat. Her name was Jean. She had her nails perfectly painted and her hair was dyed blonde and cut in a bob that stopped right below her chin. She wore just a touch of make-up. It seemed like she might be the owner.

Jean introduced herself to me and took my drink order. I would love to get a cold beer, but I needed all of my bearings so I just ordered water. I looked through the menu, and they had some terrific-sounding burgers. The difficult thing was deciding on just one.

Jean came back with my water and set it down in front of me. "Are you ready to order?"

"Kind of," I smiled and then continued, "but I can't decide which burger to get."

"Well, my favorite is the Burgundy Burger. It's a third of a pound of meat topped with mushrooms sautéed in burgundy sauce, caramelized onions, and swiss cheese. I would get it medium-well."

"Sold. I'll take it exactly as you described."

"You won't be disappointed."

I gazed out the window at the traffic passing by on Main Street. This town belonged on a postcard. If I looked beyond the stores and restaurants on the other side of Main Street, the White Mountains loomed in the background. I wondered if the people who lived here ever stopped noticing how beautiful it was. I don't know how long I was looking at the mountains, again my mind went blank, but it only seemed like a minute since Jean walked away and there she was with my order. "The Burgundy Burger medium-well."

"Thanks, Jean." My mouth watered; I had not eaten much these past three months. The burger was huge and I wondered how I would possibly finish all of it. Once I took my first bite, though, I was hooked.

Half of it was gone when Jean came over. "How is everything?"

"You were right. This is the best burger I've ever had."

"I'm glad you enjoyed it. Can I get you anything else?"

"Not right now, but if you have any ideas on a place I could stay, I would love to hear it when I'm finished."

"I'll be back in a few minutes. I have an idea for you."

"Thanks," I said wondering if she knew of any dives around here. That's all I was really planning on, anyway. Just a little hole-in-the-wall kind of place that could be my home base.

I ate all of the burger and all of the fries that came with it. I was stuffed, but I felt strong and ready to start my quest.

Jean came back with my check. "I'm not sure what kind of place you are looking for, but a close friend of mine owns a farmhouse bed and breakfast with horse stables. They have about a hundred acres of riding and hiking trails. The ski season is over so the rates are a bit lower."

My heart sank. A bed and breakfast. But something drew me to the place. I'm not sure what it was. Maybe the horses reminded me of home. Maybe it was Jean; she reminded me of my mother, and if the owner of the bed and breakfast was a friend of hers, she must be nice, too. Before I knew it I blurted out, "I'm looking for my wife."

A surprised look came over Jean's face, but also one of recognition. "Dan Gallagher?"

Now it was my turn to be surprised. "Yes, how'd you know?"

"Your accident has been big news up here. The mystery of your wife's disappearance really had people on edge for a while. It's such a strange set of circumstances."

The word "had" echoed in my head. I pulled out a chair for Jean. "Please, sit down. Look, I don't even know where to start or what I am doing here. I'm not sure what I'm looking for and I don't know what I'll find. What were the news reports?"

"First was the disappearance of your wife and the search for her in those two days before the huge snowstorm hit. In the beginning it seemed like the police thought maybe she was abducted. Then, after the snowstorm, the story seemed to turn to an accident that left your wife helpless." I noticed that Jean didn't finish the rest.

"I never knew exactly what was going on outside of my hospital room. I remember my nurse telling me that I had a lot of people praying for Deb and me. I guess we really did."

"You did, Dan. Things happen up here. There are avalanches, ski accidents—a lot of that takes place up at Tuckerton Ravine. That's a dangerous place. Your story was very different."

"It feels like a story to me. It doesn't feel like this is my life."

"Look, this place my friend owns, I think it would be good for you. I could give her a call."

"Would you please?"

Jean took the check off the table. "Lunch is on the house. I'll be right back, Dan."

Jean smiled when she returned, "You're all set. Carrie has given you her best suite. You'll love it. She'll take good care of you. I wrote the directions down for you. It's on the very edge of town. It's serene and you will be able to think and unwind there. If you need anything from me, any help at all, please let me know. We have all been wondering about you, and it is such a comfort that you are here and we can have some sort of peace knowing that you're okay."

How grateful I was for that. "Jean, thank you for everything. This means more to me than I can even begin to tell you."

"You're welcome, Dan. Take care."

"I will."

———————

I sat in my Jeep looking over the directions. I was supposed to continue on Main Street until I got to West White Mountain Road, and then take that until I arrived at the bed and breakfast. The farmhouse, white with black shutters and gardens all around it, would be on the right.

The White Mountains towered in the background at each stop sign and each turn. After I was out of the main part of town, it only took a few minutes before I saw the farmhouse off to my right. It felt like home. I turned into the drive and made my way to the top. Carrie and her husband were waiting outside for me, big smiles on their faces. I turned off the car and when I got out, they walked over to me. "Dan?"

"Yes. You must be Carrie."

"I am," she said as she extended her hand, "and this is my husband, Ken." Ken shook my hand, "I'll get your bags. You go on ahead with Carrie. She'll show you to your room."

The inside was decorated much differently than my house. My mom did simplistic, early rustic-American décor, while this farmhouse was decorated with a Victorian theme. Floral wallpaper adorned the walls of every room.

Chairs with high backs flanked the fireplace in the parlor. It was very comfortable. "Carrie, thank you so much. When I decided to come up here, I pictured staying in, well, let me just say, something a bit smaller. I think being here will do me some good."

"I'm glad. Anything that you need, we will be here for you. We all want your wife found. We will help in any way we can."

"I appreciate that. I really do."

Carrie opened the door to my room. "Wow. Are you kidding? This is too much. I can't take this room."

"I'm glad you like it and we insist that you stay here. This is our slow time and it means a lot to us to have someone here who will be able to use it."

"I just can't thank you enough."

"We're the ones who are glad that you are here, Dan. We all wondered what happened to you. I'm sure that Jean told you that."

"She did."

Ken walked in with my one bag, probably the lightest luggage load he's carried. "Here you go, Dan. So what do you think?"

"This room is fantastic. Really, I appreciate your hospitality."

Ken said, "It's our pleasure. Let us know if you need anything. I know these mountains like the back of my hand. I would be glad to take you around. I know the owner of the White Pines Lodge. I'm sure he would let us take the horses out. We could cover more ground."

"That would be great. When can we start?"

"Give me about half an hour. I'll load the horses on the trailer and meet you out front."

With that Carrie smiled and closed the door behind them. I sat on the edge of the bed and considered the turn of events. I thought I might need to rest for a little bit after that long drive, but Ken's willingness to take me out renewed my energy. I opened my bag and took out my hiking boots. I put on a pair of jeans and a white t-shirt. I put my room key in my pocket and headed downstairs to the parlor where Carrie stood holding two bags.

"Ken's almost ready. I packed some water and snacks for each of you."

"Thanks, Carrie. This is great."

Ken loaded two horses on the trailer. "We're all ready."

"Thank you. I feel like I can't say it enough to both of you. I never thought that I would be searching for Deb this way. I always pictured myself walking the trails."

"It will be faster and our vantage point will be better."

Carrie handed the bags to me as I climbed into the cab of Ken's pick-up truck. As we pulled away from the house, my heart beat faster. I was unsure of what I was looking for and of what secrets the woods held. I didn't want to go back empty-handed, but I was also concerned that if I did find something of Deb's what that might mean regarding her whereabouts.

Ken kept the conversation light on the way to the lodge. From a few blocks away I could see the familiar White Pines Lodge sign out front. The last time I saw that sign, I felt excitement at what adventures our day would hold. Now, I felt anticipation. Ken pulled into the parking lot, which was almost empty. He parked far away from the front door.

We exited the truck, and as we headed toward the lodge, a figure in a cowboy hat loomed in the driveway. He waved and Ken raised his hand in return. Ken explained, "That's the owner."

"Howdy, Ken."

"Hey, Richard. Thanks for letting us come up here with the horses."

Richard turned to me, "You must be Dan Gallagher." He extended his hand. "I'm sure sorry about the terrible time you've had."

"Me too." Richard nodded his head before letting my hand go and then he said, "Ken, bring the trailer up here. Park between the lodge and the ski shed."

As Ken moved the truck, a familiar face appeared out of the lodge. "Bruce," I couldn't help but smile as he took my hand.

"Dan, you sure are looking better than when I last saw you. You healed nicely. How are you?"

"I'm doing well, considering. I never really got a chance to thank you in person for all that you did for me. What a blessing you were that day."

"We did get your thank you letter. I'm glad that you felt you had a good support system here. Things must be rough now, huh?"

"Yeah, they are."

"Hang in there. You'll make it." Bruce stood with us as Ken unloaded the horses. Bruce was a calming force on the mountain months ago, and he still had that ability. Just having him here made me more at peace. Richard and Ken saddled up the horses and put the snacks in the saddle bags.

Both horses were brown and looked almost identical, except mine had a white diamond patch between his eyes.

Ken said, "His name is Rio, after Diamond Rio."

"I like the name."

Before we started on our way, Bruce explained to both of us, "I've gone over these woods time and time again, Dan. I sure hope you find something. We haven't given up that we'll find your wife. There are a lot of us still looking. Listen, you were on the Ptarmigan Trail when you broke your leg. Come down from where the intermediate trail connects with it—that's where you had your accident. Deb would have continued down that trail to the bottom of the hill. There are several ways to go—my guess is that she took the trail straight ahead as it would have been the most logical thing to do because the Mount Washington Hotel was right in the distance."

"Thanks, Bruce. And thanks for not giving up."

"Never." Bruce handed me a map, "Okay—get out of here."

Ken and I turned toward the golf course. There was a trail to the right that went around it. I was sure Richard would appreciate our taking that over having the horses tear up the pristine greens. What a contrast to before—all covered in white. The whole place. Now everything was shades of green. As I looked at the ground from atop Rio, I noticed the leaves and brush were thick and I immediately realized how challenging it would be to find any clues. Ken was in the lead and he turned to me and said, "We're going to cross the snowmobile trails soon. The space is wide open there. We will take that and then head up to the Ptarmigan Trail."

About three minutes later, we emerged from the wooded trail into an expansive clearing that ran from the top of a huge hill to the very bottom of it. We turned the horses left toward the incline. I didn't remember this part from months ago. I was sure I crossed it at some point, either on skis or on the rescue sled. I kept looking at the ground hoping to see a piece of clothing or something that told me where Deb might have gone and where she might be.

Having the horses was a blessing. It would take too long to walk this and the height of the horses allowed us to see much more than if we were on foot. We only went a short distance before I saw a little sign with black jagged marks on it. The expert trail marking. I remembered Deb saying, "I don't think this is an intermediate trail." My heart felt like it was going to beat right out of my chest. I could barely breathe. Ken looked back at me, "Are you all right?"

"Yes."

"Let's turn here. From what Bruce said, this should take us to the top of the hill where you had your accident."

I followed Ken. With ease the horses climbed the hill that Deb and I struggled to ascend. I remembered Deb sliding back every couple of steps, and that was when she finally took her skis off and walked up the hill.

Once we were at the top, we looked back from where we came. Nothing seemed out of place, but then again Deb would not have gone back to this side. It was the other side where I watched her disappear.

Ken asked, "Does this look familiar?"

"It does. This is definitely the way we came up this trail. The hill right over there is where I went down."

We led the horses along the ridge until we arrived at the point where Deb and I stood and she said that there was no way she was going down the hill. This was where my former philosophy of trying anything once got me into such a heap of trouble. Just seeing the narrowness of the trail, the steep drop off at the right side, and the sharp turn at the bottom made me wonder where my head was that day. I had no business skiing this hill. The horses started down the slope and looking to the right side, I noticed the tree that I hit. I could still see myself sitting on the ground waiting for Deb and the rescue team to arrive, but it felt like it was some other guy. I even started to pity that poor soul who was waiting in expectation that everything was going to be okay.

Once we made the turn near the bottom of the hill, the one I watched Deb disappear around, the trail straightened. Deb must have taken this; it was the only logical way. As we continued along the straight-a-way, the trail connected to the expansive clearing for the snowmobiles. Where Deb might have gone from here, I just didn't know. I moved Rio up next to Ken's horse as he looked out over the terrain. "What do you think?"

Ken turned to me, "If you look up ahead, you can see the Mount Washington Hotel. It would be my guess that your wife would have followed any trail that had the hotel looming in the background. The lodge is so close to it that it would make sense to use that as a marker."

"Let's follow it."

After we crossed the snowmobile trails, we entered back into a wooded area. This trail was different than the one we took to get here. It seemed to go on forever, and if Deb did this on skis, she must have thought she would never get out. I imagined this trail snow-covered and on foot. Would she keep going or would she turn around and go back to the clearing? We continued on with the trail ending at the opposite side of the golf course from where we started. I could see the lodge to the left and the hotel seemed like it was right on top of us. Deb might have come out here and traveled across the course. There was a slight breeze blowing and the air was cooler coming off the golf course. It must have been brutal crossing this in snow and ice. As to not ruin the grass, again we kept to the far end of the golf course and traveled the circumference of it. Once we were back at the lodge, Ken said, "All right, we took the route we think Deb would have taken, now let's go back and travel some of the other trails."

Ken and I reviewed the map that Bruce gave me back at the lodge, and we decided to head back toward the golf course, but this time when we got to the snowmobile trail, we headed toward the top of it. We passed the head of the Ptarmigan Trail and continued up the hill. There was a trail head to the left and one to the right. Ken offered a good plan, "We need to be methodical about this. Let's stay on the right side of the snowmobile trail. That's the side where your accident occurred. We will scour that whole area first."

We chose the trail to the right, and I noted that it was marked by blue bunny hills, an intermediate trail. This might be where Deb and I passed Rommel. I couldn't tell, though. I didn't remember any of these other trails. Ken and I spent the rest of the day searching the trails on the right side of the snowmobile path. Nothing. No cloth. No clothing. No skis. Nothing. I just needed something to point me in the right direction so I would know what to do for Deb. I needed some clue.

Ken and I rode back to the lodge without saying anything. Richard and Bruce met us in the parking lot. I was sure they knew our lack of results by the look in our eyes because Richard said, "Bruce and I are going to help you tomorrow. Can you bring two more horses?"

Ken lit up. "I sure can. Tomorrow, we will search the left side of the snowmobile trail. We'll be here at seven."

We packed up the horses and went back to the bed and breakfast. Ken called Carrie and told her we were on our way. I heard him say, "No," and all I could think was that Carrie must have asked if we found anything. That "no" bounced around in my mind as Ken reassured me that everything would come together, and I acted like I believed him. I needed to keep pressing on. Tomorrow, I will find something that leads me to an answer.

Chapter 25

There are better things ahead than any we leave behind.
—C.S. Lewis

After a restless night's sleep, I got up at six, took a quick shower, brushed my teeth, and threw on some clean clothes. I made it downstairs to the parlor in just twenty minutes. The smell of coffee made me a little more alert. Ken was already at the table and Carrie poured him a cup of coffee. "Good morning, Dan. Would you like some coffee?"

"I would love some. Thank you, Carrie."

"I have some bacon and eggs cooking. Breakfast will be ready in a minute."

"Sounds great. Thanks."

Omelets, fresh blueberry pancakes, and crisp bacon. "Do you cook like this every morning?"

Ken chuckled, "Only when we have guests, otherwise I fend for myself."

Carrie rolled her eyes. "Oh, please. Every morning I offer to make oatmeal for you, but you turn me down. You don't have to fend for yourself, you just choose not to eat what I'm making."

"Well, if you would choose to make this every day, then I would choose to eat breakfast every morning."

I appreciated the light-hearted conversation; it served as a distraction for me.

"This is a delicious breakfast, Carrie."

"Why, thank you, Dan."

We finished eating and just like yesterday, Carrie handed each of us a bag, a bit heavier than the day before, "I put some extras in there for Richard and Bruce."

Ken kissed Carrie on the cheek. "Thanks, Sweetie."

To my surprise Ken already had the horses in the trailer. I shook my head. "You two are amazing."

Ken said, "It comes with the territory. When we bought this place and turned it into a bed and breakfast, we knew the only way to make it work was to get up early and stay up late. It's something we're used to doing."

"You look like you're enjoying life."

"We are. Now, let's get to the lodge."

———◆———

I was a bit more upbeat today. It was a combination of Ken and Carrie's attitude and a change that I made in mine. I knew we didn't find anything yesterday, and at first I looked at it in a negative way, but last night I realized it was also good news, too.

———◆———

Bruce and Richard waited as we pulled into the White Pines Lodge parking lot. Ken took the truck all the way up this time and parked in the same spot between the lodge and the ski shed.

As we stepped out of the truck, Richard greeted us first, "G'morning, gentlemen. We have some coffee inside if you'd like."

Ken said, "I'm good. Carrie made a fantastic breakfast this morning and I can't squeeze one more ounce of anything into my stomach."

"I'm good too, but thanks."

Rio was my horse again today. He was a good horse. I liked his calm spirit. The horses Ken had for Bruce and Richard were just as beautiful as ours. Both Bruce and Richard seemed to be experienced riders. Bruce started, "I'm going to take the lead today. The side of the trail system that we will be searching is where I was when I got the call about your accident. The trails are shorter on this side than what you experienced yesterday because the property is cut off by the road. Keep your eyes open."

Today would yield something. I knew it. Anticipation rose in my stomach. It was a good feeling, though, not like the sick feeling I'd had for the past three months. We began on the trail that was on the left side of the golf course, but instead of continuing to the snowmobile trail, we took a path that veered down a short slope. None of this looked familiar to me, but Deb and I were not on these trails. When we looked at the map to plan out our day, the trails on this side were mostly expert, so we stayed away. The horses maneuvered over the terrain with ease. Bruce looked back and shouted, "Does anything look familiar to you?"

"No, but Deb and I were never on these trails."

"That's okay. We still need to look. Maybe she took one of these trails back to the lodge. It's easy to get lost in these woods, especially when the landscape is all white."

Bruce had a good point. The Mount Washington Hotel dominates the hillside and even from this vantage point it looked like it was right on top of us. I could see how if Deb got lost and started to follow the hotel, its location could be deceptive.

We had been riding for about forty minutes when I saw a Valentine heart stapled to a tree. My heart dropped. I remembered that day—Valentine's Day weekend. All of those hearts on the trees the day before the weather turned so cold. I remembered Deb and I laughing about people drinking champagne and skiing. This seemed pretty far down to have a heart. This section was really out of the way of where most of the trails were. "Hey, Bruce."

"What?"

"Why is there a heart on that tree? The Champagne and Chocolate tour didn't take place down here from what I can remember."

"You're right, it didn't. I don't know why it's there."

My heart beat faster. *That heart shouldn't be there, big deal.* So someone stapled an extra one to a tree. If one of the staff did it, though, that's pretty irresponsible. Someone could have gotten lost or hurt following that. After a few more steps, we found another heart stapled to a tree a few feet from the other one. I looked down the rest of the trail and there was a row of hearts leading to a wooden sawhorse blocking off the rest of the trail. We gathered around the blockade and I said, "Why is this blocked off?"

Bruce replied, "This part of the trail is steep and leads right down to the road. We don't want anyone falling or skiing onto the road, so in the winter we put up warning signs."

"What about all of these hearts that lead right to this blockade? Who could have done that? Someone on your staff?"

Richard answered next. "They better not have. This wasn't part of the Valentine's weekend ski. This is too dangerous a spot for that. We kept everyone above the snowmobile trail and we took those hearts down at the end of that weekend."

I said, "Can we take the horses down the rest of the trail?"

Bruce replied, "Let's go."

I thought I looked closely on the other trails, but that was nothing compared to the attention I paid to the ground now. We made it all the way down to the road. It was possible that Rommel was waiting for a victim, and in this case it happened to be Deb. What if he used the hearts as a marker? What if he stapled the hearts to the trees on the trail leading to the road where his car was parked and then dragged Deb down the hill? This would make the most sense in order not to be seen. The parking lot in front of the lodge was too obvious. He couldn't have parked there. We dismounted our horses and looked at each other.

Ken asked, "What are you thinking, Dan?"

I shared the story and my concern about Rommel and his involvement.

Bruce surmised, "So if he has your wife and he used this trail for his escape, then this is where we might find something."

"I think so. I feel very strongly about this place."

Ken said, "Let's walk the horses back up the trail. Dan and I will look at the ground on the right side and you two keep an eye on the left side."

I could feel Rio breathing on my neck as I led him up the trail. We were only a few feet into the head of the trail when I saw a piece of metal at the base of one of the trees. "Ken, will you hold Rio? I want to see what this is."

"What do you see?"

"A piece of metal over there."

Richard and Bruce joined us on the other side of the trail and they watched as I walked a few steps off the path. My mind wouldn't wrap itself around what it really was as I bent over to pick up the piece of shiny silver. I willed it to be just a rolled-up gum wrapper that some kid must have made into a ring out of boredom. I lied to myself as I held the ring in my hand and stared at my palm. The last time I saw this ring it was still on Deb's hand as she slipped her glove on before our ski run. I took it between my thumb and forefinger and held it up into the light. "This is Deb's wedding ring."

The three men stared at each other before Ken said, "Are you sure it's your wife's ring?"

"I'm positive it's hers. We had our initials inscribed on the inside of the band."

Ken replied, "You should put it back. Let the police see where you found it and take pictures and whatever else they want to do."

Richard called the sheriff and within a few minutes two cars pulled up. The next eight hours were filled with pictures being taken, the ring being bagged and sent to a lab, and a search party being formed. I recalled standing amid the chaos watching as the search party started from the road and walked arm in arm up the hill. Carrie and Jean were there next to each other. Bruce and Ken were also part of the search party. Richard spent his time looking over maps and helping the sheriff. Bruce shared with me that this was how it was after Deb went missing before the storm. Everyone was out here looking for her. I noticed how thorough they were; I don't know how they could have missed anything. I was confident that if there was something else to locate, they would find it. For two days this was how it went. From sun up to dusk the search party combed every part of the trail system. Every inch. Nothing. The wedding band was it.

At the end of the second day the sheriff called everyone together to thank them and to tell them the search was at an end. The sheriff was a sincere man and he took me aside earlier that day and said, "Dan, we've done all that we can do. I used up what extra resources I had for this search. We've looked and looked for your wife. I'm sorry, Dan. I don't know what else to tell you. We have the phone and the ring. Both were found in two different areas. The phone was near where you had your accident, but the ring was all the way down here close to the road. We don't have any answers or any other evidence of what might have happened on that mountain. Of course we will keep this case open, and we'll let you know if anything new comes up."

"What about the wedding ring?"

"That's at the lab. Once they are finished processing it, they will send the ring back to us and we will keep it in Deb's file."

"What else is in Deb's file?"

"Well, there's the cellphone, the surveillance tape from the lodge, some written statements from people who work at White Pines, and a statement from the guy at the bar who thought he saw your wife."

"Where is that bar?"

"It's right down the road."

I shook the sheriff's hand. "Thank you for everything that you and your staff have done. All of the help you gave me back in February when I was still in the hospital, and now all of this, I just can't thank you enough."

"I'm sorry things didn't turn out differently."

"I know. Me too."

<hr />

In the parking lot, Ken and Carrie by my side, I stood as people came up to me and gave me words of encouragement. I was amazed at how generous people had been with their time and energy. After I had my accident, I got to know a few people, mostly at the hospital, but it seemed like everyone in town knew me. With each hand I shook and with each kind word I could feel my strength returning to me. That hole that was filled with despair was being filled with hope. I still had an ache in my chest, but I was going to go on. I knew I could make it, and somehow, I would find Deb. I would have answers to all of my questions and I didn't care how long it took.

We watched as the members of the search party got into their cars and drove away. It was like seeing a line of little fireflies wind down the road and when the last one was out of sight, I turned to Ken and Carrie. "You both have done more for me than I could ever have wanted. I don't know how I will ever repay you for what you've done for me. The room, the meals, the horses, and then the search party for the last couple of days."

"Dan, there's no need to thank us; you're part of our family now. We want all of this to work out for you."

"I feel the same way about you. You are sincere through and through, and you give me hope that this will all work out."

The three of us drove back to the bed and breakfast. Ken and Carrie wanted me to stay one more night, but I couldn't. I needed to get home.

Getting out of the truck, I said, "Listen, I'm going to head out tonight."

Carrie was the first to respond. "No, Dan. Please stay tonight. It will be too late for you to drive home."

"I know it's late, but I need to get back home. The suite is beautiful and the bed comfortable, but I've been here long enough and I won't be able to sleep anyway."

Ken said, "We understand. But even if you get a few miles down the road and change your mind, come on back."

"Thanks."

While I packed up the few things that I brought with me, I thought back to the past few months about the ache in my chest, about how every turn, every path, every trail left me with a broken heart. All of this time and I still didn't have any answers. It was like I was still back on that mountain and I didn't know when I would ever get off.

I forced a smile on my face as I headed downstairs. Carrie and Ken were in the parlor, and Carrie had a bag for me. "Here are some things for the road." She gave me a hug and Ken took my hand. They walked me out to my car and when I looked back in my rearview mirror, they were still standing there, Ken with his arm wrapped around Carrie's shoulder.

Before I started for home, there was one more stop I needed to make: the bar. As I drove by, the White Pines Lodge sign was lit up, but everything else was dark. I forced myself to keep my eyes straight ahead. I didn't want to see this place in the dark, didn't want to imagine what it might have been like for Deb.

Two miles after the lodge, I saw the bar on the right. The outside was covered with wood shingles and it had a few windows with neon beer signs in them. The parking lot was huge and the gravel kicked up under my tires as soon as I pulled in. This was where a local thought he might have seen Deb. I just needed to be here for a little bit, talk to the bartender, see if he knew anything.

As soon as I opened the door, I could hear music quietly playing from the jukebox in the far left corner. The bar was a big rectangle in the middle of the room. There were a few patrons scattered around it. I walked half way around the bar so that I could see the door and most of the room. The bartender asked me what I was having. "Ginger ale."

He set it in front of me. "You look familiar. I saw you today at the search."

I stretched out my hand, "Dan Gallagher."

"Man, I'm so sorry about all this."

I had been hearing that a lot lately. "Me too. Listen, I got word that a man who was in this bar thinks he saw my wife the day she went missing. Do you know anything about it?"

"Yeah, I was here that day."

My heart jumped. "You were?"

"I was here that whole day and the next. One of the locals who comes in quite a bit thought he recognized your wife after he saw her picture in the paper. The cops interviewed me about it."

"I didn't see the report. What did you say?"

"The woman who was here that day didn't look enough like your wife did in the picture that was in the paper. That's why I didn't come forward."

"Can you tell me anything about this woman, though? The way she looked? Did she look scared?"

"No."

"Was she with a guy?"

"No."

"Was there anything that you noticed about her?"

"Like what?"

"I don't know. Just anything that you can remember. Anything."

"Let me think. She was sitting one seat to your left."

I looked at the stool and I imagined Deb sitting there alone and cold. *What happened to you?*

"Hey, Dan."

"Yeah, I'm sorry. Go on. What do you remember?"

"She was different than the typical person we get in here."

"How?"

"She looked like she didn't belong here."

"How so?"

"I don't know. Even though she had on a huge, dumpy coat and had a hat pulled down pretty far, she looked like she was from Hollywood. An actress or something. Her face was striking."

I removed my wallet from my back pocket and pulled out our wedding picture. "Was this her?"

"Gosh, she sure is beautiful. That might have been her. I'm sorry, but if the woman hadn't had that hat on, I would be able to tell you for certain."

"No problem. Thanks for your time."

I put a five down on the bar and walked out to my car. I kept going over what the bartender said, "An actress or something." There were pieces that I just couldn't fit together. There was something I was missing and for the first time since Deb disappeared, I thought maybe I was hanging onto a hope that wasn't there.

Chapter 26

I never knew the dusk could break my heart
So much longing folding in
I'd give years away to have you here
To know I can't lose you again.
—Fernando Ortega

The Fourth of July. Our anniversary. I sat by the stream and in a few hours I would be able to see the local fireworks display lighting up the sky above the tree line. I looked around the property and remembered when the back yard was filled with wedding guests. I had traveled broken heart trail long enough, and frustration finally took its toll. I put my head in my hands and let the tears come.

I heard a car door shut behind me and then another. I turned around to see Mark with Nancy by his side. I wiped the tears from my face.

As he got closer, Mark said, "You didn't think we would leave you alone on this day?"

I met them halfway and Mark gave me a bro hug, while Nancy gave me a much more tender one and said, "How are you?"

I was sure my eyes were red from crying and by the look on Nancy's face I figured she noticed, while Mark was totally oblivious. Having her share in my pain eased some of my burden. "I'm feeling pretty good. I've been doing physical therapy on my leg and that has been going well."

"How is everything else?"

"You know—some good days and some bad."

Mark chimed in, "Come on, let's get this party started. Sit down, you two."

Mark had already made himself comfortable in one of the chairs. Nancy left the chair in the middle open for me and sat. It was a beautiful night, and I let all of my troubles fall away with the tears I cried earlier and just enjoyed the present company of my friends.

I spent the rest of the summer doing two things. First, I went through all of the pictures of Deb. I put some in frames and placed them on the mantle and on the end tables in my living room. Each day I looked at the pictures and thought back to the things she said and the way she said them. I tried to recapture the smile on her face, the tilt of her head, the sound of her voice. Then, when I felt I stored enough of those memories, I took my nightly ride by Rommel's house.

Chapter 27

I will be your knight in shining armor
coming to your emotional rescue.
— The Rolling Stones

School started that year like it did every other year: football games, half-time shows, pep rallies. The scents and sounds of autumn in the air. The first day of school was the hardest, actually bringing myself to walk in. It was tough, but as I pulled in the parking lot a familiar car was parked next to my regular space. Nancy. She had waited until I arrived at school, and her support and kindness gave me the strength to walk through the doors. Each day got easier, but I spent a lot of time alone. Nancy was given her own room right next door to me, so I started to refer to her as "the girl next door." The first time I called Nancy that, she laughed and said, "I may be the girl next door, but it still feels like you're my Roomie." I suppose "Roomie" is going to stick. Nancy and I had a lot of the same students fall semester. Both of us agreed that this year's class was one of the best groups we'd ever had.

About two weeks into October, Nancy popped into my room for her usual morning visit, but she had a serious look on her face. "Hey, Dan. I need a favor."

"Well, what is it first? I don't want to agree to anything horrible."

Nancy lightened up. "Mark was supposed to chaperone the Renaissance Faire with me, but he has a job interview and can't make it now."

"Whoa, whoa, back up. Mark has a job interview?"

"Yes."

"Where?"

"At a landscaping place. He's really excited about it. He said, 'It has potential.'"

"Wow. Can I ask you a question?"

"Sure."

"I mean, I don't even know how to ask this, but you and Mark, um, am I missing something here?"

"What do you mean?"

"Are you and Mark together?"

Nancy burst out laughing. "No. I needed some help, and I knew he would pitch in. Considering he was, as he puts it, 'between jobs,' I knew he would be available. I would have asked you to chaperone, but I thought this wasn't a good time, but now that Mark can't do it, I feel differently. Let's get you out. We make a good team and I really need your help."

"When is the trip?"

"Friday."

"This Friday?"

"Yes."

"Today's Wednesday."

"I know. That's why I really need you. I'm in a bind."

The pleading look in Nancy's eyes made my heart go

out to her. I put aside the inconvenience this meant for me. "Okay, I'll do it."

"Thank you, thank you."

"You're welcome."

"Listen, would it be too much to ask you to wear a knight costume?"

"What?"

"Well, we all dress up for the contest."

"Contest?"

"The costume contest. If all of the students and chaperones dress up, we win a prize. Mark rented a knight costume."

"Nancy, I'm not dressing up."

She looked a little dejected. "I know it's a bit much. It's no problem; I'm just glad you'll be there."

That night Mark showed up at my door holding the knight costume. "Hey, I bought an eye patch for it."

"An eye patch?"

"Yeah. I wanted to be a pirate, but Nancy said that I had to match her and she made me be a knight. I decided to be a knight with an eye patch. I bought a sword, too."

"You're crazy. I'm not wearing that thing."

"I know, I know. Just in case you change your mind."

"Don't hold your breath. So, Nancy said you have an interview on Friday."

"Yeah."

"That's great, man. I'm really happy for you."

"I figure if I ever want to get my life in order, you know, have a real relationship with a woman, I should have a job."

"That would be a good start. Is Nancy the one that made you feel this way?"

"Nancy's great, but she's not interested in me. Trust me; I tried."

"Oh, really?"

"Yeah, I even went in for a kiss."

"You didn't."

"Please, brother. Of course I did. Nancy was like, 'What are you doing?' She totally shot me down. Anyway, we talk once in a while. I told her to keep an eye on you."

"Is that why she stops in my room every day?"

Mark winked. "She would have done that without my suggestion."

———————

By the next day the students that Nancy and I both taught heard that I was chaperoning, so all morning long I fended off questions about what costume I was wearing. The students had it all planned out. Some were going to be knights, others were going to be peasants, while many of the young ladies were going into princess mode, like Nancy. I asked, "Is anyone going as a pirate?" Three hands went up. The hands belonged to three of the biggest guys in my class, all football players. Our football team had been struggling this year, and one day during class someone mocked our losing record. It was a stupid thing to do considering the student who said it wasn't on the team and was no match for the three young men who were and who sat right behind him. Before anyone else could chime in, I gave a speech about courage. I said something to the effect, "When life knocks you down, you get back up. Our football team gets on the field every day after school to practice, and no matter what happens that Friday night, they're back the next week. That's courage and that's perseverance, and they deserve our respect." Ever since then, those three guys acted like I was their best friend.

I added, "Pirates? At the Renaissance Faire?"

One of the "pirates" responded, "Absolutely. They even have a pirate show. Come on, Mr. Gallagher, dress up. It'll be fun."

"I do have a knight costume at home."

"Cool. Wear it Mr. Gallagher."

The bell rang and as the class departed I kept hearing, "Please, Mr. Gallagher."

So that night I tried on the costume. Black tights with black leather shoe covers that looked like boots, a black velvet tunic with a gold lion on the front and gold stripes around the arms, and a black velvet cape with gold underneath. I liked almost everything, but I couldn't get past the tights, so I put on the eye patch. Much better.

Nancy had done more for me than anyone else, and really all I ever did was act like a selfish jerk. I took and took in this friendship and gave nothing back. Every year our school won an award for the costumes. I would do this for her. Tomorrow, I would show up at school dressed like a knight and finally start acting like a true friend.

———

Mental note—take off the eye patch before pulling up at the drive thru. When the woman behind the window looked at my eye patch, she said, "Ahoy, matey."

I said, "Actually, I'm a knight."

"Sorry, my mistake."

That wasn't to be the only time that day I was to hear that phrase. As soon as I walked into the school, that's all I heard. The three pirates were so excited that they met me at my door. "We just wanted to see if you would wear a costume. Hey, we can be the Four Musketeers. We all have swords and eye patches, except we're pirates and you're a knight."

I taught my first period class until eight o'clock, and then we were dismissed to meet the buses in the back of the school. All of my students were going on the trip, so I locked my door and headed outside. Nancy was already there directing who belonged on which bus. We had two full bus loads of students, probably about one hundred. The day was gorgeous with a high, blue sky that looked like it could go on forever and served as the backdrop for all of the leaves turning yellow, orange, and red. Nancy told me that I had the first bus and she would take the second. Nancy dressed like a princess wearing a pink gown and a long pointy hat with material billowing out of the top of it. "Nancy, you really went all out on your costume. I have never seen a real princess, but I can only imagine you're as close as it gets. Is the costume comfortable?"

"Not at all. Hey, you look fabulous. Thank you so much for dressing up."

"Ah, you're welcome. I didn't want to let you down."

"I knew you wouldn't." Nancy smiled, "It looks like everyone is ready. Let's go."

The three pirates were on my bus. I claimed the front seat and they sat in the surrounding ones. For one entire hour I heard constant attempts from them to imitate the pirate language and accent, if there is such thing as a pirate accent. They referred to us as the Four Musketeers, saying, "Arrrrrrr," each time. It made me smile.

We arrived at the front gate, which looked like the entrance to a castle. A representative from the Renaissance Faire climbed up the stairs onto the bus and in a perfect English accent said, "Well met."

The students all followed with, "Well met." They sounded pretty good, too.

She continued, still in her perfect accent, "Hear ye, hear ye. All cellphones, iPods, mp3 players and any other electronic devices must stay on the bus. They would be an anachronism since electronic devices do not belong in the Renaissance. So ladies and gentlemen, without further ado, let us go back to a much simpler time."

The three pirates filed off the bus, wooden swords raised above their heads, shouting, "One for all and all for one."

The grounds of the Faire were decorated with pumpkins and gourds. At the entrance was a huge pumpkin man. Most of it was made of straw and wire and pumpkins. It was actually a little ominous and I couldn't help but stare at it. Nancy waited for me right in front of the pumpkin man. "Hey, Nancy. This thing's a little creepy, wouldn't you say?"

Nancy looked up, examining the hollowed stomach cavity with pumpkins spilling out of it. "A little." She turned back to me, "We're all set. The students are meeting us at the mud pit at one o'clock. That will give us plenty of time to get back to school for dismissal."

Nancy handed me a copy of a performance schedule. "We need to check in at the chaperone tent first, but look over this and see if there are any performances that you would like to watch. There are also some cool shops that you might like to visit."

⚬

The schedule listed performances of Shakespeare but also a sword swallower. A definite must. Also recorded in the line-up were student performances and other contests besides the costume contest scheduled for noon. We had a lot to pack into just four hours, lunch included.

Nancy handed me a cup of coffee and after taking a sip of hers said, "I'm ready. What do you want to go see first?"

"Why don't we go see the sword swallower?"

"How did I know that would be your first choice? Anything you want, but I'm warning you, it might make you feel sick."

"Ha, ha. I have a pretty strong stomach. I think I'll be fine."

We wound through the cobblestone streets, stopping in a shop filled with lawn statues and ornaments. A grapevine served as a roof over the pathway to the inside of the shop. Glass balls and wind chimes hung from the grapevine. A woman dressed in a black cloak greeted us. There were a few things here that would be great to place by the stream, but I didn't feel like lugging around a piece of concrete or-namentation. After we left the shop, we visited a place filled with essential oils, at least that's how Nancy explained it to me. She smelled each of the oils, trying to choose one for her signature scent. Passion was a good one, but evergreen was definitely out. Nancy settled on passion. The owner of the shop put the oil and a bottle of lotion to mix with it in a small bag for Nancy. We continued on our way, passing a bookstore and a loose-tea shop before coming up to the Main Stage Theater where the sword swallower was performing.

<hr />

The sword swallower certainly drew a big crowd because there were no seats, and by seats I mean little wooden benches sitting on top of dirt. Nancy and I stood near the back and watched the show over the top of the crowd. Let me just say that Nancy was right about the sick thing. She had been here quite a bit more than I had, and I should have listened to her. When the sword swallower gave a warning that his show might make some people feel ill, I almost laughed out loud. Come on. But, after a very long explanation of how not to try this at home, when I watched him stick a sword down his throat, I began to gag. Nancy muffled a laugh, but the more I gagged the harder she laughed. We had to leave. Thankfully, we stood in the back so we slinked out unnoticed.

Nancy confirmed, "I told you it's gross. I can only take it because I've seen it so many times."

"I still can't believe that made me gag. Knights don't gag."

"Maybe we should head over to the joust where a true knight belongs. That shouldn't trigger your gag reflex."

"Well played, Nancy."

The day went by quickly. Before we knew it, twelve fifteen arrived, the costume contest was over, and we were taking home first place. Nancy was thrilled and could hardly contain herself. As we talked about which show to see before we headed out, we passed three of the Musketeers, who yelled across the way, "Ahoy, Mr. Gallagher. We're off to the pirate show. We need the last Musketeer with us."

I shrugged my shoulders while Nancy agreed, "Let's go."

We followed our students to the pirate show. The pirate set was made to look like a ship. It had three levels, each with ropes, windows, and trap doors. This show was full, too, but there was one bench in the front that had space for all five of us. I sat on the end, Nancy was next to me, and the Three Musketeers were on the other side of her. We talked for a few minutes and then a woman wearing a long, blonde wig and dressed as a pirate swung out on a rope from one of the levels above us and jumped down to the ground stage level. "Good Afternoon, Ladies and Gentlemen."

Even through the noise of the audience, that one voice echoed in my ears. As she confidently closed in on the audience, I saw past the pirate's costume and blonde wig to the brunette hair that I was used to seeing spread across her pillow at night and to the piercing blue eyes that used to greet me each morning. All of these months that I spent looking for her and Deb was here. Safe. I stood up and from the side of the stage I heard, "Ahoy, my lady," only to see a pirate with long brown hair drawing his sword. I froze. Rommel Hagan. Deb was still addressing the audience and as she turned to where I stood, we made eye contact and I barely heard her whisper, "Dan." With fear in her eyes she turned to the pirate next to her. I had waited for this moment, the moment I met Rommel face to face, the moment I made him pay for all of the pain he caused. I drew my sword, rushed the stage and yelled, "Rommel Hagan." As I swung my sword at Rommel's head, stage hands appeared at his side. I kept swinging, and before I knew it, the Three Musketeers were next to me fending off the extras. All I wanted was Rommel. I didn't know what he did to Deb or what happened on the mountain, but I was going to make him suffer for all of it, and as I raised my wooden sword his metal one met mine, cutting it in half. I threw it to my side while my students continued swinging theirs. Nancy yelled, "Dan! Stop! Boys, get back here!" The audience applauded and as Rommel made a run for it, I heard someone say, "This is the best pirate show ever. The fighting seems so real."

Thanks to the Three Musketeers, I freed myself from the encircling stage hands and chased Rommel and Deb through the standing ovation of the audience and onto a cobblestone path leading to the mud pit. Nancy and our students ran behind, some in anticipation and some in disbelief. The mud show was still going on as Rommel, Deb, and I ran on stage. The pit was in front of us and the audience cheered as I charged Rommel, knocking him into the thick mud. Deb jumped in and bellowed, "Get off of him." Rommel stood up, and my right fist met his left cheek, knocking him back into the mud. Deb screamed once more, "Leave us alone," and grabbed my arm before I could hit Rommel again.

"Leave *us* alone," I repeated, holding onto both of her arms.

She pulled away. "You?" she shrieked at me.

Confused, I said, "You? What do you mean, 'you'? Deb, what are you talking about?" All the pain and anguish of searching for her these eight months flowed into my entire being all at once and I had to stop myself from being consumed by it. "Do you have any idea how I've looked for you?" Then I remembered the search party and all of those wonderful people who came out in the freezing cold and then a few months later into the scorching weather to look for her. "Do you have any idea how many people have looked for you?"

Deb mocked me, "Ha, well I've been here the whole time." Rommel cowered off to the left of her, looking like he was ready to take off if I made the slightest move.

"What do you mean 'You've been here all the time'? You need to help me understand this. I've spent eight months looking for you. I didn't know if you were alive or dead. I didn't know if you were being tortured or were hurt or what."

"Well, I'm fine."

"What are you doing here?"

"Who cares now? You're fine and we can all go on with our lives."

"My life is with you."

"My life isn't with you. It's with Rommel. You have no idea what a woman like me needs. You may think that your life is with me, but you live in a dream world. My life certainly isn't with you. It never was."

"Not with me? Who then, this scum? I did everything for you. I gave you anything you wanted and you know what, you didn't even have to ask because there I was stepping in again and again doing whatever I could to make you happy."

"Well, I wasn't happy. This life is better."

"How is this life better? What kind of things do you have here?"

"I have the man I love."

"The man you love? This piece of garbage?" I pointed at Rommel. It was my turn to yell, "You live in a tent. How is that better?" I wound up my right fist as far as I could, but before I could punch Rommel again, the Three Musketeers came running through the mud yelling, "All for one and one for all," and knocked him back into the mud. Even though there was a huge crowd around us, there was total silence as security moved in and began to clear everyone out of the mud pit. Nancy said in a quiet voice, "Everyone to the buses. Now." The students started their way across the park. I looked back to see Deb tending to Rommel, both of them covered in mud. That would be the last time I would ever see her again.

I turned back to Nancy and tears welled up in her eyes, "Dan, are you all right?" She reached out to take my hand.

"Nancy. Don't do this now. Don't cry. I can't take it."

Nancy took hold of my arm and steadied me. "You can do this, Dan. You're fine."

"I have to stay until the police get here."

"I'll be waiting back at the buses with the kids."

I took a deep breath and watched the princess make her way through the crowd, followed by the Three Musketeers.

⸻

It didn't take long for the local police to arrive and after interviewing all three of us, the police informed Rommel that he was listed as a person of interest and would be taken into custody. Since Deb was a missing person, she also had to go to the station. The police allowed me to call Joel, and after he explained everything to them, they let me go.

<hr />

As I took the lonely walk back to the bus, the day's events flashed through my mind. The mud started to dry and I could feel my skin tightening. I'm sure they were not, but it seemed like everyone in the park was staring at me. As I got closer to the buses, I held my head up. Nancy waited outside the bus and standing side by side next to the bus doors were the Three Musketeers, holding their swords ceremonially above their heads. I walked underneath, entered the bus and took my seat in the front. Nancy returned to her bus, and the guys came in, sat behind me, and we started our journey home.

We rode back to school in silence. When we pulled up to the back of the building, I stayed in my seat. I didn't move, but as each student passed by me, he or she put a hand on my shoulder without saying anything. The Three Musketeers were last and they handed me a piece of folded paper. I tucked it in my pocket, and before I could make it down the steps, the bus driver stopped me. "Hey, I just wanted to tell you that those three boys dressed like pirates, well, when they got on the bus they said that if anyone took any pictures or videos of you they would find out and personally take care of them. They had your back, and, um, I'm also real sorry about what happened."

"Thanks."

"Take care, Mr. Gallagher."

Our students had enough time to go back in the building and get their things. Nancy approached me, "Dan just go. It's Friday. No one will care—I'll cover for you."

"I think I'll take you up on that," I said as I walked across the parking lot to my Jeep. I put the key into the ignition and pulled away so I didn't get stuck behind the buses.

During that car ride home, I was glad to be alone. All of my emotions came out; I hadn't cried like that since my parents passed away. I pulled into my driveway and noticed Joel calling me on my cellphone. I sat in my car and listened to the bizarre tale. Joel told me that Rommel, the coward that he is, totally ratted Deb out. It was all her idea. She loved Rommel, but they barely made any money even between the two of them. Rommel agreed to let her find a man with money, marry him, and then eventually divorce him, getting as big of a settlement as she could. She would then take the money, and Deb and Rommel would live happily ever after. Deb thought she had found just that man in me. When she saw the horse farm, she thought she hit pay dirt, but when Rachel threw in the prenuptial agreement, that changed things. Deb was going to walk away, but then the life insurance policy enticed her. She asked Rommel to be patient, that they would get their chance to take me out. During the two years we were together, Deb never really went on tour; she was with Rommel each time. Even the days before our wedding, Deb was with him. That explained the tears. She didn't want to leave him; it had nothing to do with her friends. No wonder no one from her side attended the wedding. She probably didn't even send out invitations. Rommel knew, though, and the truck parked outside my house the morning of our wedding was his. He sat there as long as he could until he realized that Mark saw him, and then he drove away.

Joel proceeded to tell me about that day on the mountain. Rommel was sick of waiting after a year, and Deb started to feel a little nervous about their plan. That day we were skiing, Rommel was there to kill me. I'm not sure how they were going to do it, but when I had my accident, Deb saw it as an opportunity to walk away and let me freeze to death, so there would be no way to trace a homicide back to them. She never thought I would be rescued. Once Deb disappeared around the corner, she put her skis back on and followed a trail that Rommel marked with hearts. It led to a road where Rommel had a snowmobile parked. As they drove back up the trail, Deb threw her wedding ring into the woods. They came back near where I was to make sure I hadn't been rescued. That explained the motor I heard that day. I knew it was a snowmobile; I just had no idea it was my wife running off with another man, leaving me for dead. Then they rode to the bar where Rommel's car was parked. They went inside to have a celebratory beer, but they went in separately so no one would tie them together. Deb was wearing Rommel's coat to keep warm, and she had her hat pulled down so she couldn't be identified. After they exited the bar, they left the snowmobile in the parking lot and took Rommel's truck all the way back to Pennsylvania. A few days later Deb was sure I had died of my injuries, so she went to my house with Rommel to pick up some of her things, only to their shock, I was home on the living room sofa. They broke in to kill me, and I was glad I had the sense to grab the shotgun out of the closet. Joel said the shotgun pellets grazed Rommel and scared both of them so they never came back to the house. Their plan was for Deb to find another guy and do the same thing. Joel said, "I'm not sure exactly what is going to happen to the two of them, but they won't be getting away unscathed. I'm sorry to have to tell you all of this."

I hung up the phone, and still caked in mud I walked into my house through the living room and without stopping picked up the fireplace poker and smashed every one of the pictures I put up of Deb. Glass flew everywhere and crunched under my shoes as I made my way to the back door. I dropped the poker on the patio and while walking outside to the stream, I took off my clothes and found the deep water in the bend. I let the current take away the mud that was stuck in my hair and splashed all over my face and hands. While under the water, I heard a muffled cry in the distance. I came up for a breath and saw a beautiful princess standing along the bank, calling my name. Nancy. She had been there for me through all of this.

Nancy cradled several towels, a blanket and clean clothes. She held a towel up for me. "You should get out now." The water was so cold that it numbed my body. While I walked toward her, Nancy held my gaze. How many times had I looked her in the eyes these past few months? But never like this. As Nancy wrapped the towel around my waist and put the blanket around my shoulders, I pulled her toward me, finally realizing my true princess had been with me all along. We stared into each other's eyes, and I held her face in my hands and kissed her. We stood for a minute looking at each other.

Nancy turned, scooping the muddy knight costume up in her arms. She started back to the house and I said, "Looks like Mark won't be getting his deposit back." The corners of her mouth turned up in a smile.

I rested on one of the Adirondack chairs. I don't know how long I sat there before I felt a hand on my back. Nancy didn't say a thing; she just sat on the arm of the chair, and as earlier in the day, steadied me with her presence. Nancy handed me a piece of paper. "I found this in the pocket."

It was the note the Musketeers handed me earlier. I opened it and read familiar words:

> *When life knocks you down, you get back up.*
> *That's courage and that's perseverance.*
> *You have our respect.*
> *See you Monday, Mr. Gallagher.*
> *—The Three Musketeers.*

See you Monday. "You know, Nancy, I prayed that Deb was okay."

"And God answered your prayer. All of your fears and bad dreams, all of the wondering and searching; it's over now. You're not on that mountain any more, Dan."

"It took me eight months to get off that mountain." I pulled Nancy onto my lap and kissed her again. I examined her dress, her hair, her eyes. "I always thought it was the knight in shining armor who was supposed to rescue the princess."

Putting her arms around me, Nancy whispered in my ear, "Roomie, you did."

www.ingramcontent.com/pod-product-compliance
Lightning Source LLC
Chambersburg PA
CBHW071851220626
47052CB00002B/68